I0831514

AWKWARD IN PRINT

AN AWKWARD NOVEL

RACHEL RHODES

Awkward in Print

Rachel Rhodes

First published 2019

Cover design by Apple Pie Graphics

Edited by The Writer's Block

George's office is so big that I feel like I've been marooned in an ancient leather chair on an island of mahogany hardwood. Citrus and Old Spice wage an aromatic war with the lingering cigar smoke in the air. I find myself flicking my foot so that my sandal flaps against my heel. Flap, flap, flap, a steady beat counting the seconds.

"Jojo." George peers at me over his glasses. An impatient smile, a small gesture toward my feet. "Would you mind?"

"Sorry." I stop flapping and start to bite the edge of my thumbnail instead. I should have known not to arrive on time. George never runs to schedule and so, thanks to the ingrained punctuality my father drummed into me from my first day at kindergarten, I have spent the last ten minutes trying not to fidget while he reads the final pages of my manuscript. I'm not a writer. If I were, I would probably feel a sense of pride instead of this crippling sense of anxiety. I can even pinpoint its source. It's tucked between pages 243 and 244.

George wheezes out a chuckle, a combination of thirty Marlboro a day, and what I hope is the joke I made in the final paragraph. He removes his glasses and fixes me with a watery-eyed smile.

"Fabulous!" he announces, dropping the manuscript on the desk before him with a hefty thud. I can't help but think that if we'd stuck to the cold hard facts, it would be significantly less effective – possibly a single sheet of paper wafting gracefully down onto the broad surface. "Poignant, endearing and sincere," George continues, and I can practically see the dollar signs reflected in his pupils. "We'll release in six months, to coincide with the film premiere."

F u u u u u u c k.

George presses a pudgy thumb onto the PA system resting on his desk. The button is worn, greyed in the center where it was once black.

"Yes, Mr. Beresford?" Sally's switchboard-smooth voice purrs through the intercom. I try not to remember the time I walked past her unattended desk and into George's office to find her servicing George rather than the copier. I've not been able to look George's saint-like wife, Susan, in the eye since.

"Sal," George booms. I wonder why he bothers with the intercom when she can clearly hear him through the door. "Approve Jojo's proofs, the polish is perfect. I want a bound print proof on my desk next week."

"Absolutely, Mr. Beresford."

I suck in a breath that doesn't reach my chest.

"George," I begin tentatively, "I'm not sure if we're one hundred percent ready. Some of the stuff in this book has been exaggerated, and—"

George cuts me dead. "Of course it has. Nobody wants to read the memoir of a celebrity who hasn't done anything wild or crazy. Everybody does it." At the word 'everybody' he opens his arm to indicate the framed photographs behind him. Gina D, Lucy Cale, Harrison Wentz, all boldly emblazoned with signatures and messages of thanks. George Beresford: Agent to the Stars. Paula Power addressed hers to 'Big George'. I shudder to think what that means and make a mental note to send Susan a fruit basket the second I leave this office.

I take another deep breath and try again. "But say someone had to discover that the truth has been... tweaked. Wouldn't that be grounds for a lawsuit?"

"A lawsuit? Jojo, you've been watching too many movies." He bellows at his own joke and then flips to page two of the preliminary pages. He jabs at the text midway down the page. "This," he tells me, "is a disclaimer. It indemnifies you against any such claims. It also," he lowers his voice conspiratorially, "allows us to blend as much fiction into the memoir as we please, without consequence."

"Okay, but legal consequence aside, I have my reputation to consider."

"Reputation? Jojo, that's *my* job. Besides, there's nothing like a scandal to ensure a meteoric rise to stardom. Not that you need it," he adds quickly. He's right, I don't. Right now, I can command more money than Julia Laurence, a fact she pointed out when we lunched last week. I'm officially the highest paid actress in Hollywood, surreal as that is. George didn't choose me, I chose George. Because, in the shark-infested waters of Hollywood agents, George is a nurse shark. Still...

"I don't know if I'm quite comfortable with that..." I begin, but he cuts me off again.

"There's only one thing in this book that matters. We even built the title around it, for God's sake. Jojo, you are a *virgin*. A real-life, twenty-six-year-old, celebrity virgin, living in L.A. You're as rare as it gets. In fact, if someone discovered a living, breathing dinosaur, we'd still outsell them."

I'm pretty sure that's not true. I wonder if I could actually find a real-life dinosaur, while George continues. "The rest doesn't mean shit. So, unless you've gone and dropped your panties for someone between writing the first draft and getting engaged to Alex, we have hit pay dirt."

There's a pause as George waits for this to sink in.

"I haven't," I say truthfully. Then I flick my foot.

It's been six months since my last visit and Sally has put on weight. She's also put on a perpetual smirk, and she barely bothers with discretion when it comes to placing her perfectly-manicured hands all over George. I'm back in his office, marooned, terrified, and holding a copy of my book in my hands. It's gorgeous – all gold foil and embossed font. *Hollywood Virgin: the dazzling autobiography of Jojo Hudson.* George came up with the title. I wasn't so sure about the word 'dazzling'. There's a silhouetted photograph of me in the background. I'm looking over my shoulder, straight at the camera. The word 'Print' is reflected in my eye.

"I love it," I tell George, truthfully. I do love it – the cover especially. It looks like a book I would buy. That doesn't make me feel any better about it, though. For the thousandth time, I wish I'd never told George I was writing this damned book. He seized upon that announcement like it was the Academy Award of his professional life. Within a week, he'd found a publisher. Three days later I'd signed a contract. I've had nightmares ever since.

"I'm having two thousand copies delivered this afternoon. We're all set for the launch next week."

"Wonderful," I lie. "I can't wait." An air kiss later and I'm out the door. I step out onto the street and take a few gulps of fresh air. The tightness in my chest eases, but only marginally. Right on cue, my driver pulls up, double parking, to a cacophony of angry hoots. I rush forward as he opens his door.

"I'm going for a walk, Phillip, I'll call if I need you."

"Yes, Miss Hudson." Phillip slides back onto the cream leather and signals. He pulls out into the traffic without missing a beat, but narrowly missing a red Mercedes.

I keep my head down. It's become a habit but today more than any I need to be alone with my thoughts. I've managed to sweep my anxiety under the rug for the past six months, but now it's returned, with a vengeance.

"Oh my God." A low voice to my left draws my attention from the cracked sidewalk, and I turn to find a young woman behind me, hanging onto a neon-blue dog leash. I follow the line of the leash to find a squirming golden spaniel tying himself into knots.

"Are you...?" The woman frowns at me and cocks her head to one side. I wait for the moment that I know will come. Her eyes widen, and her lips part as her head snaps upright. "Oh my God, you are!"

I smile, having learned the hard way that to deny it will only lead to a scene. "I am." I keep my voice down, hoping she will follow suit. Unfortunately, today is not my lucky day.

"I can't believe it! Oh my God, I'm such a fan. Your biggest fan. Could you..." she trails off, digging inside her oversized handbag and practically throttling the spaniel in the process. "Aha!" she whips out her phone in triumph. "Would you mind if I took a selfie?"

I nod. Grit my teeth. Step forward. By the time she jabs the photo button, I'm leaning into her, a picture-perfect smile on my face.

"I'm Donna, by the way," she says, as she checks the photo.

"Hi, Donna." The smile is still plastered on my lips. I can hold it for hours; my cheeks don't even cramp anymore. "I'm Jojo."

She laughs at that. A manic, over-the-top laugh that implies my joke is the funniest thing she's ever heard. The spaniel whimpers.

"I think your puppy is in a bit of trouble," I say. Donna glances down, gives a start, and bends to untangle the puppy before it loses consciousness. I take the opportunity to slip into the crowd of pedestrian traffic walking down the street. I feel a bit bad for pulling a vanishing act on Donna, but I've learned from experience that it's easier to cut and run. At least she'll always have that photograph. As I walk, I tie back my hair with the elastic band around my wrist and pull a pair of enormous Prada glasses from my bag. I walk three blocks without a single person recognizing me. Dark glasses and messy buns have saved my sanity more times than I can count.

I'm almost at *The Office* when my phone rings. My smile is genuine as I answer.

"Hey, babe!"

"Good morning beautiful." It's his I-just-woke-up-and-I'm-horny voice, not to be confused with his I-just-woke-up-and-I-want-to-cuddle voice. Alex and I had been dating for two years when he proposed. We've been engaged for just over a month, and some days I still have to pinch myself to make sure I'm not dreaming. Only just turned thirty, handsome as the devil and one of the youngest people ever to make the Forbes World's Billionaires List, Alex Masters is quite easily Hollywood's most eligible bachelor. That is, he was, until he met me. Automatically, I glance at my ring finger, where a five-carat diamond flashes brightly in the sunlight.

"How did the meeting go?" Alex yawns down the phone. Up all night working again, I think fondly.

"It went well. George is happy with the final edits."

"So, you're still on for the launch?"

I fake an enthusiasm I can't bring myself to feel. "We are!"

A pause. Alex is nothing if not intuitive. I catch my bottom lip between my teeth.

"Well that's good news," Alex says eventually. "I'm proud of you, angel."

That familiar warm feeling washes over me. "Thank you."

"Where are you now?"

"I'm just popping in to see Jude."

"It's a bit early for a drink, don't you think? Must have been one hell of a meeting," he teases. "Don't fall in love with him." It's his standard response whenever I visit my oldest friend in L.A.

"I'll try."

"I'll see you later. I should be done by seven or so."

"Perfect, I can't wait."

I disconnect the call and step inside *The Office*, a singularly inappropriate name for the small, low-lit bar. At this time of the morning, it's completely empty.

"Well, as I live and breathe, if it isn't Miss Josie Hudson!" Jude's familiar grin flashes in my direction from behind the bar. Jude can't resist calling me by my real name, even though almost everyone else has adopted my stage name. Everyone but Jude, my sister, Teddy, and my parents. He's wiping down the counter, his blond bed-head sticking up in all directions. I dump my bag on top of the counter he's just cleaned.

"What can I get for you, Miss?" Jude asks. My chest relaxes completely at the sight of the familiar devilish glint in his eye.

"Don't you start." I whip off the dark glasses. "I need coffee."

"You know where everything is," he says, but I'm already moving behind the counter, toward the coffee machine.

"You want one?" I ask over my shoulder.

"Make it a double. I had a hens party in here last night which just wouldn't leave."

Jude goes back to his cleaning while I whip up two coffees with the skill and ease of someone who spent three years working behind this bar.

I carry the two chipped mugs back to the counter, slip back around it and take a seat on one of the well-worn bar stools. Jude drops the cloth to take the seat opposite me.

"So, how did it go with King George?"

I take a sip of my coffee. "We're all set."

"Nice. You must be excited."

"Mmmm," I mumble, non-committal.

"Do I get to come to this fancy launch party you're having, or will George have a shit fit if you bring in the help?"

"Of course you're invited! You *are* coming, aren't you?" I fix him with a hard look, daring him to say otherwise, and he holds up his hands in mock surrender.

"I'm coming, I'm coming!"

"Good."

Jude doesn't let me off that easy. "I don't really have anything to wear."

I throw the cloth at him.

We settle into a comfortable silence. *The Office* hasn't changed much in the three years since I stopped working here. When I first arrived in Los Angeles, Jude was the only person who'd give me a job. He'd treated me kindly, kept my chin up when I failed to land any roles, encouraged me to keep auditioning when I was ready to give up, and advanced my pay-check when I couldn't make my rent. Without him, I probably would've scuttled back to Bridgeport, Connecticut with my tail between my legs before the first year was up. As it turns out, it was a good thing I didn't. My breakthrough role was a small part in an indie film that went on to win two Independent Spirit Awards. One for Best Feature. The other for Best Supporting Female. The first was our debut director's first award. The second was mine.

Within six months I landed the role of a lifetime. Primera Pictures were looking for a female lead to play the role of Hollywood legend Greta Garbo, in a feature film based loosely on her life. I got the part. I also got myself an agent – George.

"Oh, before I forget," Jude breaks the pensive silence and rummages beneath the counter. He withdraws a magazine and slaps it onto the counter before me, narrowly avoiding upending my mug. "I saved you this. I'm sure you'll want as many copies as you can get," he adds.

Alex's handsome face stares out at me from the cover. It's not the first time he's been featured in Times magazine, but it is the first time he's made the cover. The black and white photograph doesn't capture the hazel of his eyes, or the lighter streaks in his dark hair, but there's no denying the hard line of his jaw or the bold chin.

"You're going to drool on it," Jude teases, sliding it away from me. I slap my hand on the cover, hindering his progress and he lets out a low chuckle. "Take it, please. If I catch sight of him staring up at me one more time when I'm digging around under the bar, I'm going to throw up. He's like the fucking *Mona Lisa,* those eyes follow me everywhere."

"Oh, stop it. You know you love him."

"I wouldn't go that far. But so long as he's making you happy, he's got my vote."

I finish my coffee and make to carry the cup around to the back, but Jude stays me with a hand. "Leave it, I've got it."

"You sure?"

"You don't work here anymore, remember?"

"You know, sometimes I wish I did. It's true!" I insist as he laughs out loud. "I had fun here. It was like spending every day with family."

"Speaking of family – how are your folks?"

"Good. Dad just upgraded his truck."

"He didn't!" I laugh along with him. Jude knows as well as anybody that my father is frugal to a fault.

"Mom broke down at the store, and he finally caved."

"And Teddy?" his voice changes when he asks after my sister and I give him a knowing smile.

"Teddy just broke up with Scott number 2, so if ever there was a good time to call her..." I let the suggestion hang between us, but Jude shakes his head.

"I've told you a thousand times. It's too complicated."

"And I've told you a thousand times that I have no problem with you dating my sister. God knows she could do with a good man in her life."

My sister's full name is Theodora. Mine is Josephine. Our

parents are as traditional as they come, but fortunately, in an act of extraordinary kindness, our extended family intervened and never called us anything but Josie and Teddy. Teddy has spent the past five years dating two men named Scott. Not at the same time, obviously. Scott 1 lasted three years, Scott 2 only two. Neither deserved even a second date, but Teddy is nothing if not determined. Jude has had a thumping crush on her since the first night they met, but he refuses to act on it.

"It's not just you," he says now, "although that's certainly a big part of it. There's also the fact that we live on opposite sides of the country."

"Teddy's a vet. She could move."

Jude laughs. "I own a bar, yet you expect your sister to give up a thriving private practice?"

"Teddy needs adventure in her life. She's too comfortable. That's why she sticks it out with losers, because she's allergic to change."

"Exactly. Now stop plotting. I'm perfectly happy being single." I know that he is, but that doesn't stop me constantly trying to play matchmaker. Realistically, I know that he and Teddy as a couple is never going to happen, so I'm constantly trying to set him up with people right here in L.A. Jude changes the subject pointedly. "When does filming start?"

"The week after next."

"How many people are coming to the launch?"

My heart quickens at the mention of the dreaded event. "I'm not sure."

"Any pretty single ladies for me to flirt with?"

"Actually, I do have a—"

"Don't you dare, Josie I was joking. I'm not interested."

"But—"

"But nothing. I'm not into those Hollywood types." He realizes what he's said an instant before my face falls. "Shit, I didn't mean it like that. You're... well, you're different. But could you really imagine any of your actress friends hanging out here, in this place?" He spreads his arms wide to encompass the entire bar.

I smile. "More's the pity for them," I say, leaning forward to kiss his cheek. "They don't know what they're missing. This happens to be my favorite place in the world."

I could swear he's actually blushing. I scoop up the magazine and fold it under my arm. "I'll see you later, Jude."

His reply reaches me as I reach for the door. "Later, Josie"

3

"Good afternoon, Miss Hudson." Frank, my doorman, greets me as I step into the air-conditioned lobby of my building.

I flash him a smile. "Hey, Frank. Any messages?"

"No, Ma'am."

I keep walking toward the elevator. "How many times have I asked you to call me Jojo?"

"Company policy," he reminds me, for what must be the hundredth time. "Have a wonderful evening, Miss Hudson."

I wave at him as I step inside the elevator and press the button for the penthouse. "You too, Frank."

Other than *The Office*, my apartment is my favorite place in the world. It spans the entire top floor of the building, and the roof access leads to a private garden, complete with rim-flow pool. After the initial viewing, I had been captivated, and my sister Teddy had talked me into making an offer.

"You deserve it," she'd insisted when I'd balked at the price, "and besides, you can afford it. You know you can."

And I could, so I did. Since then, my finances allow for me to move to any of the sprawling mansions in the Hollywood Hills, but I just haven't found the inclination to leave. I have purchased three additional apartments in the same building, two of which I rent out. I keep the third for private guests.

Alex and I haven't properly discussed where we will be living after the wedding, but from the way he speaks, I've gathered that we will be moving into his home in Calabasas. Whether or not he expects me to sell my apartment, I have yet to figure out.

I drop my purse on the table in the hall and slip off my sandals as a frenzied yapping erupts in the kitchen. A ball of caramel and white fluff skids around the corner and launches itself at me.

"Hello Noodle," I croon, scooping her up. Noodle is a mixed breed mongrel I found injured on a set two years ago. Her back leg had been badly broken, and she'd spent four weeks in a splint, after which I'd had to take her for hydrotherapy twice a week for another six. After going through all that, there was no way I was giving her up. Unfortunately, she's not an endearing dog, and she hasn't got the looks to make up for her bitchy nature. Not even her vet can hazard a guess as to her breeding, but he's pretty sure there's Pomeranian in there.

"I thought that must be you." Fenn, my personal assistant, is standing in the doorway to my office, smiling at Noodle, who is now running laps around my legs. At twenty-three, Fenn is four years younger than I am, but she's efficient and reliable, and I wouldn't survive without her. Even Noodle tolerates her, and Noodle hates everyone.

"How did the meeting go?" Fenn asks.

"It went well. We're all set."

"I thought as much. Should I go ahead and consolidate the RSVPs?"

"Do it tomorrow. Why don't you knock off early and surprise Seb?"

At the mention of her boyfriend, Fenn grins. "He's taking me to dinner. Alejandro's," she adds shyly. No matter how many fancy restaurants Fenn attends with me, she still seems overwhelmed when it occurs outside of her line of work.

"Oh wow. What's the occasion?"

"I have no idea."

My eyes widen. "You don't think...?"

"Oh, hell no! I'm only twenty-three, Jojo!"

"True, but you and Seb have been dating for a while. You never know."

"Trust me, *he* knows better."

"Well, whatever the reason, Alejandro's is no simple date. You should look your best." I give her a meaningful look.

Fenn grins. "Really?"

"I insist."

She follows me through the apartment to my bedroom. My walk-in closet is almost double the size of my bedroom. The upside of being a Hollywood star is that you are never at a loss for designer clothing. The downside is that you need somewhere to keep it all.

It takes Fenn twenty minutes to make up her mind, a steady pile of discarded satin and lace mounting on the pale grey carpet.

"It's perfect!" I announce when she finally stops long enough to admire herself in the full-length mirror. The Naeem Khan dress sits mid-thigh on Fenn's long legs, the stark black-and-white geometric pattern softened by the gauzy fabric. Shoulder cut-outs end in black-ribboned ties just below the elbows. It's not too formal, but dressy enough for Alejandro's.

"I love it," Fenn admits. I help her braid her auburn hair over one shoulder and with an expert hand, I touch up her make-up.

"Shoes," I say when we're done. Fortunately, we have the same size feet. She picks out a pair of black leather ankle boots, and I approve.

"Leave it," I say when she starts to clear away the mess. "I'll get Ursula to do it in the morning."

"Liar." Fenn knows me too well.

I roll my eyes at her. "You're going to be late."

"I promise I'll look after it," she says as I usher her to the door.

"You can have it. It looks better on you than it ever did on me."

She opens her mouth to argue, but I'm already closing the door. "Have fun!"

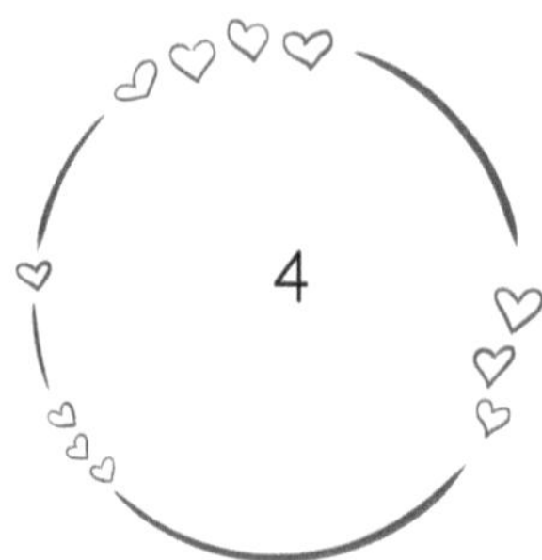

4

By the time Alex arrives, I've tidied up and poured myself a glass of perfectly chilled white wine. I hear his keys hit the table in the hall a nanosecond before Noodle begins her frenzied yapping from the safety of my lap.

"Hush!" I give her a gentle shove off the couch She gives a dramatic yelp and jumps right back up.

Alex breezes into the living room and gives her a wry frown.

"Not today then?" he says. My stomach drops as his eyes find mine. His dark hair is slicked back, still damp from a recent shower, and the olive polo-neck he's wearing brings out the yellow flecks in his hazel eyes.

"Not today," I agree, scratching Noodle behind the ears. Every time Alex visits, he claims one day Noodle will decide he isn't so bad. It's been over two years, and he's still confident. He reaches out a tanned hand and pats her head.

"You will love me, Noodle," he says in a hypnotic voice. Noodle growls at him.

"How was your day?" I ask, pushing Noodle aside as he flops onto the couch beside me. She gives him a baleful look and then leaps off the couch to settle in her basket with an air of martyrdom.

"Long," Alex says. "I had back to back meetings. Which reminds me, I'll be out of town next week. I have to fly to Munich on Monday morning for a bid meeting. Don't worry," he adds teasingly, catching sight of my horrified face, "I'll be back on Friday morning, in plenty of time for the launch."

"Oh, thank God. I need you there."

He pulls me against his chest. "As good as it feels to be needed, did you honestly think I'd miss it?"

I reply by kissing him. It's long and lazy, but too soon, my blood is thundering in my head, and my fingers are moving up and under his shirt of their own accord.

Alex pulls away, breathing heavily. "God, I can't wait to marry you." He shifts a little, obviously uncomfortable. I get to my feet and offer him my hand.

"Let me help you with that," I grin, my eyes flickering to the bulge of his pants. We may not have had sex yet, but I can certainly ease his discomfort.

Later, we eat at the kitchen counter. It's casual and comfortable.

"God, Ursula is an incredible cook," Alex sighs. "I never knew a simple salad could taste this good."

"I know." I pop another caramelized onion tartlet in my mouth, and the pastry dissolves on my tongue. "Why do you think I'm so intent on bringing her with me when we're married?"

"You better watch it, love. They say the way to a man's heart is through his stomach, you know."

"Really?" I tease. "And the way to a woman's?"

His eyes sparkle. "Through her pants, obviously."

Before he leaves, Alex asks me to play for him. The Baby Grand piano I picked up at Sotheby's after my first big paycheck has pride of place in the white living room, but I haven't touched it in weeks. I've played since as long as I can remember. It was the reason I'd been accepted into Julliard in the first place. After one year, I'd migrated into the four-year acting program, because I'd realized that while music was my first love, acting would be my last.

"I haven't warmed up," I moan, but Alex is merciless.

"You don't need to. I'm tone-deaf, remember?"

He's not tone-deaf. He never has been, but he loves to hear me play. I take a seat on the piano stool I had custom-made when I bought the Baby Grand, and flip open my songbook.

"No," Alex groans. He hates it when I play by the book. I stick my tongue out at him, but I close it anyway. My fingers rest on the ivory keys for only a moment before the first movement of Beethoven's *Moonlight Sonata* comes to mind. I've always found this particular piece heart-stoppingly beautiful. At some point, Alex gets up to stand behind me, his strong fingers trailing the very top of my spine, lifting my hair, which has long escaped the bun, out of the way, but I barely notice. The music carries me away, as it always does.

I open my eyes when the music ends.

"Beautiful," Alex whispers, leaning down to drop a kiss on the top of my head.

When he's gone, I play the third movement. It couldn't be more different from the first – the technical piece a true workout for my unpractised fingers. I cringe at every wrong note, but I play through to the end, and when I finally head to bed, I sleep like a baby.

CEECEE GETS to her feet when I arrive at our usual table. "Jojo!" My name becomes an entire song when CeeCee says it, and I disappear into her cloud of perfume as she pulls me in for a hug. CeeCee kisses both cheeks, even though she's not French. Her real name is Cecily, and she grew up in a trailer park near Pittsburgh, but God help anyone who mentions it. At five foot two, she's diminutive, but I've seen grown men cry when faced with her legendary temper. CeeCee likes things to go her way.

"I took the liberty of ordering champagne," she announces as we take our seats. Immediately, a hovering waiter steps forward to fill my glass.

"It's only ten o'clock," I point out, filling a second glass with iced water. The waiter frowns at me as though by not asking him to do it I've caused deep offense.

"Yes, just too early for wine," CeeCee muses sadly. "So!" Her braceleted hands clap together. "Fenn mailed me. Everything is ready for the launch? How divine, darling, you must be thrilled!"

I take a hearty slug of my champagne. "I am."

"Well, I sent out all the invites we agreed upon, and a few extra last-minute to press we hadn't considered before. Everyone is coming, obviously."

"I have no doubt." I pity the press who try to deny CeeCee Cooper.

"Now when can I get my hands on a copy of the book?" she asks. "You know I've been dying to read it. Stuffy old George wouldn't let me take even a peek at the unpolished manuscript, but you know I want a signed copy."

Slug. "You'll get one, I promise."

"Wonderful. Now, what are you going to have to eat?"

I already know what I'm having – fresh tuna salad with no dressing – so while CeeCee deliberates over the menu, I scan the balcony. Two women in matching suits are having a heated argument. A woman with a bouncing baby boy on her lap is giving the man across from her bedroom eyes. She's wearing a wedding ring, and he isn't. A blond man with a short, military haircut is...

"Shit!" I raise my menu so fast it slaps me in the nose.

"What?" CeeCee squawks.

"Nothing," I say, keeping the menu raised. "There was a bee."

CeeCee's hand snaps forward and yanks the menu from my grasp. I spare a quick look back at the balcony, but the man is gone. I must have been imagining things.

"A bee?" CeeCee asks dubiously.

"Yes." I take another huge swig of my champagne. "It must have flown away."

By the time I leave the restaurant, I'm wobbling on my legs. It takes me forever to locate my car.

"Are you alright, Miss Hudson?" Phillip asks as I fall onto the leather seat.

I wave away his concern. "I'm fine, Phillip." I reach into my purse and root around until I feel the expensive tissue-lined envelope. "Could you drop me at *The Office*, please."

It takes me three tries before I manage to open the door to Jude's pub. When it finally opens, it's so unexpected that I almost fall flat on my face. From behind the bar, Jude bursts into laughter.

"I thought you'd be stuck out there all day," he says.

"Oh, shut it." I make a concerted effort to walk in a straight line, but I still end up three feet to his left. I slide right. "Your invitation, Sir," I announce cordially. Jude takes the invite from my outstretched hand. "So, you have no reason not to attend."

"Where the hell have you been?" he asks as he tears it open.

"I had breakfast with CeeCee."

"Jesus, Jojo. You should know better. The girl grew up with truckers who ran an underground gambling ring. She could drink Old Man Farley under the table."

Old man Farley is one of *The Office* regulars. He comes in every day, Monday to Saturday and drinks until Jude cuts him off. He doesn't speak. Ever. According to Jude, the first time he'd come in, he'd simply pointed to the bottle of single malt on the bar, and that had been that. We started to believe he might be mute, until one Saturday evening when Jude refilled his whiskey, and out of the blue he'd asked why Jude didn't open on Sundays. Jude had been so shocked the whiskey had overflowed.

"Jude goes to Church on Sundays," I'd whispered gravely in Old man Farley's ear. It was easier to lie than to explain that even Jude needed one day off a week. He'd never spoken again, but he could drink for the U.S.A if ever they made it an Olympic sport.

"You're probably right," I say now. Jude taps my nose with a long finger.

"You need coffee."

I don't even offer to help as he sets about making us both a cup.

"You need to RSVP," I tell his broad back.

"To the invitation you handed me fifteen seconds ago?"

"That's the one."

"I already told you I'm coming."

"I thought you might change your mind. Once you've got the invitation, your RSVP is official."

He sets the mug down in front of me and grins. "Why are you so worried about me coming to this shindig anyway? I hardly come to any of your premieres anymore, and it doesn't bother you."

"This is different. It's my first book."

"Do I have to read it?"

I throw a metal coaster at him. It misses by a mile.

"I'm coming, Jojo. You can take this as my official RSVP."

"Thank you. And you're welcome to bring a date."

"Great! I'll ask one of the hundreds of women who beat down my door on a daily basis."

"Ouch."

The downfall of owning *The Office* and spending almost every waking moment keeping it running, is that it leaves Jude very little time to date. It also means far too much time being pawed by lady patrons who have had too much to drink. It doesn't help that he's incredibly easy on the eye.

"You could always bring Laurel," I suggest helpfully.

"I could," he agrees wryly, "if I was in the business of breaking the hearts of beautiful girls."

That's the thing about Jude – he's just all round too nice. Laurel was my replacement when I left, and she fell head over heels in love with Jude within the first two weeks on the job. Laurel is beautiful. An all-American girl with blonde bangs and a shy smile that can melt even the lowest tipper's heart. She's perfect for Jude, in every way except one. He's just not that into her.

"I guess it would give her the wrong impression," I sigh, then, in a flash of inspiration, "what about CeeCee? She's single! And you certainly wouldn't have to worry about breaking her heart."

"Because she doesn't have one?"

I slap his arm.

"I'm joking! But still, no. Thanks, Jojo, but I'd rather go on my own."

"Oh, come on! You and CeeCee get on fine. She's gorgeous, and I know she finds you attractive. You deserve a night of guilt-free, meaningless sex."

"Oh really? And what would you know about that?" He's teasing, but I blush to the roots of my hair. I've never actually told Jude the truth, but he figured it out anyway. At least, I think he did. It's hard to say for sure.

"Cat got your tongue, Jojo?"

"No. I'm trying to formulate an argument."

"Ah," he nods his head gravely. "Not so easy to do when you're tanked."

"True. I still think you should go with CeeCee."

"So I can have guilt-free, meaningless sex?"

"Yes!"

"You're adorable when you're shit-faced."

I stay with Jude until I'm sober enough to navigate the sidewalk without an escort.

"Home, Miss Hudson?" Phillip asks.

"Yes, please."

I rest my head against the window, the cool glass heaven against my flaming cheeks. Jude's right, CeeCee *is* a terrible influence. We take a left turn, and I watch the people waiting for the light. A streak of dark-blond hair, and then we're passed. I whip my head around, but it's impossible to see anything through the crowd gathered on the sidewalk.

"Are you alright, Miss Hudson?" Phillip asks, more amused than concerned.

"I think I'm seeing things," I mutter, and then, before he can ask me what, I quickly add, "I may have had a bit too much champagne at breakfast."

"That's nothing two Tylenol, a big glass of water, and an hour-long nap can't cure," Phillip replies helpfully.

I decide to take his advice. Fenn doesn't bat an eyelid when I tell her I'm not feeling well and that I'm going to lie down for an hour.

Noodle is less impressed, especially when I lock her out of the bedroom.

"I'll take her for a walk when I take my lunch," Fenn promises.

"Thanks, Fenn."

I lie on my bed and close my eyes, willing sleep to come. Sleep does no such thing. Instead, I replay the two sightings of the blond man over and over in my head, trying to recall if at any point I got a clear view of his face. *No,* I scold myself. *You didn't. You're just thinking of him because the book is about to launch. Go to sleep.*

"Jojo?"

I jerk awake with a start.

"Sorry!" Fenn apologizes sheepishly. She's poked her head around my bedroom door. "I just thought I should let you know I'm headed out." I glance at my watch. It's after three. I slept the entire afternoon.

"Are you feeling okay?" Fenn asks.

"Yes, I'm fine. I took some pills, they must have knocked me out."

"Okay, well I took Noodle for a walk. Ursula is still here, so I've left her in the kitchen. She's cooking something which smells heavenly. Do you need me to get you anything before I go?"

"No, I'm fine. I'm up."

"Then I'll see you tomorrow."

"Hey, you didn't tell me about your date."

"It was dreamy. No proposal, thank God, but the dress was a hit."

"I'm glad to hear it."

She flashes me a grin. "Enjoy your evening."

"You too."

I hear the receding click of her high heels on the tiled floor, and I slump back onto my pillows. I start filming the week after next. It's exactly the distraction I need. I just need to get through the launch first.

"OH MY GOD, Jojo, it's even better than I expected!" George booms in my ear. It's incredible how, when one is dreading something, time seems to fast-forward. The week leading up to the launch was a blur, and now, here I am, in a stunning black Vera Wang dress, my heart in my throat. George and I are crushed together in a sea of bodies, under an ambient light that makes everyone beautiful. "Everybody is here," George continues as a waiter struggling to hold a silver tray aloft squeezes past. George helps himself to a crab cake with one hand, while the other caresses the red satin of Sally's ample behind.

"Where is Susan?" I ask pointedly, trying not to look.

"She's here somewhere," George replies airily. "No doubt checking that the caterers haven't run out of crab."

"Isn't that *your* job?" I ask Sally. She gives me a look that could melt metal, but I hold her gaze defiantly. I'm an A-list Hollywood actress. She hasn't a hope in hell.

"Don't give Sal a hard time," George whines as Sally stalks off to stuff her face with buffalo wings.

"George, I love you, but I swear to God if you don't at least try to be discreet, I'm going to fire you as an agent. Susan is a saint."

"I never said she wasn't." He's so remarkably unapologetic and so naturally charming, it's impossible to stay mad at him.

I roll my eyes. "I don't know how she puts up with you."

"I'm incredibly well-hung. Now you better get your sweet ass over to the signing table, the queue is already halfway across the room."

"You've left grease stains all over Sally's ass," I say as I march off.

"You look like a woman on a mission." I raise my head at the sound of Jude's voice.

"I wondered where you were!"

"Did you think I was going to chicken out?"

I shake my head. "Never."

He holds up a copy of my book. "Can I get your autograph?"

"I was actually on my way to the signing table, but I suppose I could save you the wait."

He laughs as I scrawl across the title page. Jude takes it back and looks down at what I've written. He smiles when he sees I've signed it, *With Love, Josie* instead of Jojo.

"I like it," he says.

"Are you going to be around for a while?"

He looks over his shoulder at the length of the line. "You're going to be at it for hours. I'm probably going to head out."

"But you just got here! We haven't even had a minute to chat!"

"We can do that this week. You've got a busy night ahead."

"Fine," I grumble. "I am glad you came, though."

"I told you I wouldn't miss it." He kisses my temple and disappears into the throng.

I take my seat at the massive table and pick up the *Waterman* pen George gave me especially for tonight, my name engraved in the silver. George is a shit, but he's the best agent in the business, and I trust him. He gives his clients all the respect and attention he fails to give his wife.

"Jojo, look this way, please!" a reporter calls and then I'm off, posing for photographs and signing books until my wrists cramp. The line is never-ending.

"You look like you could use a break."

I look up to find Alex standing before me, a proud smile on his face, a copy of the book in his hand.

"You bought it?" I laugh. "I have a dozen copies at home!"

"I'm supporting my girl." He holds up the book. "And I want it signed, this is going to be worth a lot of money one day."

I take it and scrawl in the title page, covering my words with my free hand so he can't read them.

"Alex, Jojo!" A photographer calls. "This way, please!" Alex leans toward me, and the man gets his frontpage photograph.

"How much longer do you think I'll have to do this?" I ask.

Alex looks over his shoulder. "You're just about done. I'll buy you a drink after." A wink and a flash of white teeth and he's gone.

The line is definitely coming to an end, but if I never sign my name again, it'll be too soon. I barely look up as the next person in line steps forward.

"Could you personalize it?"

My head snaps up. All the air is driven from my lungs and my smile, which has never faltered in all my years in front of the camera, dies on my lips.

"Ace." It's a whisper, but he hears me.

"It's nice to see you again, Josie."

Oh God, that voice. That deep, husky, sex-is-mandatory voice. His face hasn't changed much. His blond hair is shorter, cropped close to his head, and a few lines crease the skin around his eyes when he smiles, but he is still staggering. His arms are broader, more tanned, and the blue silk shirt he's wearing is a perfect match for his eyes.

"You'll sign it, won't you?" I'm staring. I drop my gaze, cheeks flaming to find his hand on the table before me. He's holding my book. *Holy fucking hell.*

6

"Ace, what are you doing here?"

The book is still in his hands. I don't want to touch it.

"What, I can't support an old friend?" His eyes dance with amusement. He's enjoying the fact that he still makes me nervous. *Bastard.*

"I wouldn't exactly call us old friends."

"Then what would you call us, Josie?" It's a challenge, laid down bold and bare.

"Acquaintances. At best."

"Everything okay here?" George appears as if by magic and manages to smile at Ace and frown at me at the same time. "There are still a few people waiting, Jojo."

"We're almost done," I tell him. Satisfied, George wanders off in the direction of the food table.

I snatch the book from Ace's hands. My fingers brush against his, and I swear I feel sparks fly where our skin touches.

"You can't have this," I tell him firmly.

"And why is that?"

"I..." I lick my lips and stumble for an excuse. "I just don't want you to have it."

"I've paid for it."

"I'll reimburse you."

"Excuse me, is this going to take long?" A raven-haired woman leans around Ace to ask. Then she catches sight of his face. A red-taloned finger comes to rest on his shoulder. "Sorry," she purrs, "I don't mean to rush you."

Ace shrugs. "That's okay." He yanks the book out of my hands. "I'll wait until you're done."

The rest of the signing is a blur. All I am conscious of is the fact that Ace has moved to the back of the line and every autograph brings him closer to the table. My pen tears through paper as the raven-haired woman saunters to his side and engages him in conversation. Her lipstick is the same color as Sally's dress.

"I'm so sorry," I tell the person whose book I just ruined. I pull another from the display pile at the edge of the table and sign it. "Here you go."

"I can't wait to read it," the next person in line tells me. "I'm such a fan!"

"Thank you so much. I hope you enjoy it."

"Could you possibly sign it to Tiffany?"

"Sure." I scrawl her name in the top right corner. Red lips is smiling up at Ace, her body arched toward him.

Sign. I've lost sight of them.

Sign. He's smiling back.

"Who is Josie?" a man in a grey pinstripe suit frowns down at his signed copy.

"Sorry!" I snatch it back and pull another copy from the decorative pile. "Here you go."

Finally, there's no one left.

"Let's try this again," Ace asks, stepping up to the table. The woman stands just behind him, waiting for him to finish. Ace turns to her, and I catch a whiff of his cologne.

"Sweetheart," he drawls lazily, "why don't you go and get yourself a glass of champagne. I'll meet you at the bar."

I swear if a lioness looked at a stag the way she's looking at him right now, it would die a blissful, pain-free death of testosterone overload. She sashays off in the direction of the bar.

"Give it back," I snap, refusing to look at him.

His voice is nothing like it was when speaking to the lioness, all trace of charm gone. "Why don't you want me to read it?"

"I just don't." I feel pricks of shame in the corners of my eyes, and I swat them away.

Ace braces his hands on the edge of the table and leans forward, so close that our noses are almost touching. "Does it have anything to do with chapter twenty-seven, Josie?" he asks.

I can't breathe. I jerk away from him, my back slamming into the back of my chair.

"Jojo?"

Oh God, oh God. Alex. Alex is here. He's standing next to Ace, a concerned expression on his beautifully familiar face.

I try to sound normal. "Hi."

Wrong. He knows me too well. Alex is sizing Ace up, and Ace hasn't moved. He's still crouched over me, his hands splayed on the table. No wedding ring.

"I'm almost done," I say, giving Alex a reassuring smile. He hesitates, torn between his need to protect me and making a scene in front of the entire Hollywood press.

"I think George wants you to start the interviews," he tells me. "I'll wait right over here." He moves away, but not far enough that he can't keep an eye on me.

Ace still hasn't moved.

"Please," I whisper. I don't know what I'm asking.

"We're not done," he replies. "Meet me tomorrow at *Gerard's*. I'll be there at eleven."

He takes his unsigned book with him.

By ten thirty the following morning I'm a bundle of nerves. My deepest darkest fear has literally become a reality. I take a cab to *Gerard's*, rather than let Phillip drive me. The subterfuge makes me feel even worse. The inside of the diner hasn't changed. I haven't been here in years, but it's still a popular college hangout, judging by the patrons. I slip into the red leather booth at the very end. I make sure to sit facing the wall, but I still tug at my beanie.

A frazzled waitress sidles over. "What can I get you?"

"Coffee, please. Black, no sugar."

"Anything to eat?"

"No, thanks."

My untouched coffee grows cold on the table. I check my watch. It's 10:56.

"You want another?" the waitress asks, looking at my full cup with a puzzled expression.

"I'm okay for now, thank you. I'm actually meeting someone, so I'll order another when he arrives."

She gives me a knowing look. "Got it. Just call me if you need anything."

The bell above the door jangles.

"Hey stranger!" the waitress calls. "Where have you been?"

"Would you believe it if I told you I'd gone off coffee?" I'd know that voice anywhere.

"Not in a million years," the waitress laughs. "She yours?"

I cringe, imagining Ace looking at the back of my head.

"Sure is," he replies easily. "Could you bring us two coffees, please, Marla?"

He's getting nearer, I can sense him, and then a denim-clad leg appears beside me.

"Hello Josie," his voice is softer than it was last night, more coaxing. He drops into the seat opposite me, larger than life. He's wearing a black sweater, V-necked and form-fitted. I've never seen a simple sweater look that good.

"Why am I here?" I ask. I'd already decided the best defense is a good offense, especially where Ace is concerned.

He frowns at me. "You're not going to ask me how I've been? What I've been up to these past six years?"

"I don't care."

A cup thumps onto the table before me. Perfect timing that Marla should arrive just in time to hear me say that. I keep my eyes lowered, terrified she'll recognize me if I look up.

"Here you go," she says, setting Ace's cup down far more gently. "You want anything to eat, John?"

John. It was so easy to forget his real name. Ace had started the first week of college. There were three Johns in our class. Usually, the lecturers would simply call them by the last names, but in this case, King and Jackman had been too good an opportunity to pass up. Ace's last name is Logan, but he'd become Ace. Ace, King and Jack. The joke had led to the three becoming friends, and they were seldom seen apart for the remaining three years at Julliard.

"I wouldn't mind a big plate of French fries. You want anything, Josie?"

"No, I'm good."

"Just the fries, then."

As soon as she's out of earshot, I try again. "What do you want, Ace?"

He takes a swig of his coffee. "Hardly anyone calls me that anymore."

"You must be devastated."

He stares at me over the rim of his cup. "When did you become so bitter?"

"Bitter? I'm not bitter, Ace. You ambushed me at my book launch, threatened me, and now I'm here, with no clue why. Forgive me if I'm not thrilled about it."

"If you're not thrilled now, wait until I tell you why you're here." It's a threat – implied, but a threat nonetheless.

"You read my book."

"I did. Last week actually." I don't bother asking how he got his hands on a copy when the book was under a worldwide embargo until last night. What would be the point? I can hardly file a lawsuit against the person who leaked it, not without revealing how I know and the reason I care. "It was good," Ace continues, "you're a good writer. A better actress, and an even better pianist, but the writing was solid." I don't have anything to say to that, so I keep quiet. When he speaks again, his voice is like silk. "Chapter twenty-seven, Josie?"

"My name is Jojo."

"You're deflecting."

I slam my hands down on the table. "What do you want me to say?"

"I want you to tell me why you lied."

"That's none of your business."

"I think it's very much my business."

"Why?" I sneer, anger radiating off me in waves. "Because you screwed me once, six years ago, and now you want to cash in?"

He settles back in his seat, completely unperturbed by my outburst. A flash of pity and then he smiles. "Actually, that's exactly what I want to do."

I should have expected it, but I'm still stunned when I hear the words. Furious, I snatch up my purse.

"Fine," I say, rooting around for my checkbook. "Name your price. If it's money you're after, just tell me how much so I can get on with my life."

"I don't want your money. At least not directly," he taunts.

I stifle the urge to scream. "Then what do you want?"

He smiles again, and it turns my blood to ice. "The same thing every Julliard graduate wants. Fame and fortune."

I gape at him. Marla arrives with the fries, and he coats them in ketchup while I watch in stunned silence.

"Here's the thing, Josie. I have a feeling that this secret could seriously impact your reputation. Your fiancé doesn't know either, does he?" He stares at me in silence and I feel the blood drain from my face. "I'll take that as a yes. So... reputation, career, fiancé. All the things you stand to lose if I go to the press."

"Why are you doing this?" I would never have expected this of him. He might've been an asshole once, but he wasn't a bad person. In fact, he was probably the nicest guy I ever knew, until he wasn't.

"I'm actually doing you a solid. You have the opportunity to salvage two of those things."

Two of those things. My reputation and my career. The only two that go hand in hand.

"No." I get to my feet. "I'm not doing this."

"Sit down, Jojo." His voice is clipped, all trace of charm vanished. I don't miss the fact that he's spoken my instantly recognizable name out loud. It's another threat, clear as day. I sit.

"You want me to break it off with Alex. Why?"

He grins. "Why do you think?"

I shake my head in horrified disbelief. "Fuck you, Ace."

"Well, I didn't expect you to take it that far, but I'd hardly say no."

"You want me to dump my fiancé and become what – your girlfriend?"

"Not forever. Just as long as it takes for me to establish myself." He pops a few fries in his mouth. I feel sick.

"You couldn't cut it as an actor on your own, and you expect to make it by riding my coattails? Are you delusional? This business doesn't work that way."

"This business works exactly that way, and you know it."

"I can't make you a star, Ace. Hell, I didn't even make myself one, I just got a lucky break."

"You have a lot more power in this business than you give yourself credit for."

I give him a scathing look while I try to think of a way out of this mess.

"Fine," I concede with a sigh. "I'll help you. I'll take you to events, put you in touch with the right people... all of it. But I don't need to break up with Alex and fake-date you to do that."

"No deal. The dating part is mandatory."

"Why?"

"Remember Jack Danvers?"

Everyone remembers Jack Danvers. Second husband of mega-star Sarah Carter, Jack was a nobody. Until his raging affair with Sarah came to light.

"Jack isn't famous, he's infamous," I point out. "He may be a household name, but everybody hates him."

"Only because he broke up a marriage. Last I checked you and Mr. *Forbes List* hadn't tied the knot yet."

Inwardly, I curse having had to delay the wedding because of studio commitments. Outwardly, I give Ace the filthiest look I can manage.

"He'll never buy it," I say. "Alex won't just accept me leaving him."

"Then I suggest you make your performance believable."

I can't believe we're having this conversation. "How did you become this person? You were a good guy, Ace."

"Not good enough for you, apparently." There's a bitterness to his voice that jolts me.

"It doesn't have to be like this. We were friends, once. We can be again. I can help you, I'll do everything in my power to help you, but not like this. It's extortion."

Ace yawns.

"I love him, Ace."

"You'll get over it."

He is so cold, so cruel, that I snatch up my purse.

"Go to hell. Do your worst, I'll just deny it. Who do you think Hollywood will believe – America's sweetheart, or the bastard trying to get his fifteen minutes of fame?"

Ace picks up his phone. "I thought you might say that. Fortunately for me, I have evidence."

"You're lying."

His lip curls. "Check your email. I'll expect to read about your break up by the end of the week. And Jojo," he adds as I turn to leave. "I'm not a patient man. Don't keep me waiting."

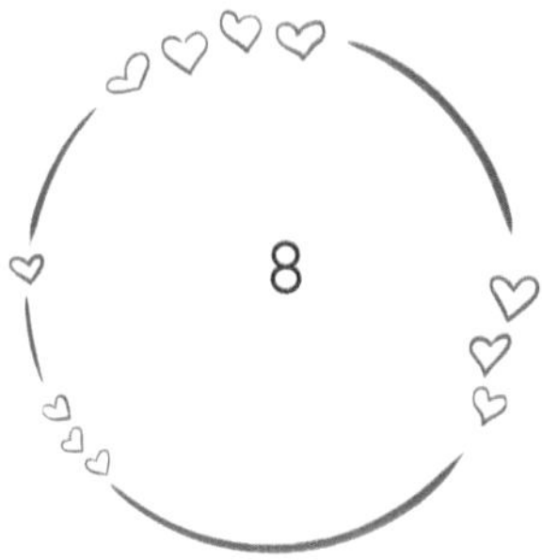

Oh my God. The photographs. We took photos. The memory comes flooding back and my face burns as I scroll through the images Ace has sent to my email. I'm lying naked in his bed, mascara smudged beneath my eyes. My hair is a dark mass against the cream sheets, and the empty Vodka bottle is visible on the bedside table. Ace is smiling down at me. The other images are taken at various times during the course of that night. We're half dressed, playing strip poker. We're doing Tequila shots, grimacing as we tear into slices of lemon. I'm dancing on a table, the result of a lost dare. In every picture, I'm gazing up at him through heavy-lidded eyes. The wanton look on my face is all the evidence he needs. I shove my phone back into my purse and lean back against the worn seat of the cab. One night. One stupid night and a handful of drunken selfies is going to destroy my entire life.

I'd been lovesick for John Logan from the first time I laid eyes on him. Even before he got given the nickname Ace. We shared a lot of the same classes, but he'd never noticed me in that way. He was always friendly – that was just how he was – but it wasn't until we'd landed the lead roles in a major production Julliard was putting on at a local theatre that I'd made any headway. We'd had to spend a lot of time together. I'd cherished every single moment. The night we wrapped, our entire senior class had turned up for the party, and I'd had far too much to drink.

"Miss?" The cab driver's voice yanks me back to the present. We're outside my building.

"Thanks." I hand him a crumpled bill. "Keep the change."

I go straight to my bathroom and splash cold water on my face. The eyes staring back at me in the mirror are hollow. My hair is lighter now, honeyed highlights softening the dark, and a smattering of faint freckles dusts my nose and cheeks. I find myself wondering if Ace still finds me attractive, and then berate myself for giving a damn.

He'd been so sweet that night. He'd taken care of me, made sure that I was looked after. He'd seen me safely home. Then he'd seen me naked. My roommate, Casey, had hooked up with John Kingman, and she wasn't coming home.

I still don't remember who made the first move. One minute we were saying goodbye, the next, his lips were on mine, and we were kissing as though we no longer needed air to survive. If he'd taken me to my bedroom, then and there, I would've let him. Instead, he'd led me to the couch, his wicked smile full of promise. We'd played strip poker. Slowly. Ace had refused to let me drink anymore. He'd taken my shots for me, until his beautiful blue eyes were crossing.

"Why?" I'd asked as I'd peeled off my top after a spectacularly bad hand.

"You've had enough," he'd said firmly. "I don't want you to regret this."

By the time I was down to my underwear, I was squirming with desire. Ace was wearing only his boxers and one black sock.

"You lose," he murmured, showing his hand.

I reached behind me to unhook my bra, but his hand closed around my wrist. His eyes bore into mine. "Let me," he whispered. It was my undoing. He was pretty drunk, and his fingers fumbled a few times, but under his expert hands, I'd unraveled.

"Jojo?"

At the sound of Fenn's voice, I whirl toward the bathroom door. I can picture her standing on the other side, checking her watch.

"Yes?" I croak.

"We need to leave now if we're going to make it on time."

THE DISTRACTION I've been waiting for is a hollow victory. Filming starts this afternoon, and this is a role I've been looking forward to for months. The movie is a dark thriller, and I play a woman who falls in love with her best friend's husband. It's my most dramatic role to date.

I spend two hours in hair and makeup and then check my phone to find a text from Alex, wishing me good luck and promising that he'll see me tomorrow morning before work. The filming schedule begins with two weeks of night work, so our schedules will be conflicting until then. I can't bring myself to reply to his text.

"Your eyes are watering Miss Hudson," my make-up artist warns. I blink rapidly a few times and close my eyes.

We work for eight hours straight, breaking only for drinks of warm water laced with honey to preserve our voices, and one light meal. The director, Harrison Garfield, is in the twilight of his career and has been around long enough that he still remembers a time when actors and actresses weren't prone to being spoilt. He's both brilliant and brutal.

"Cut!" he yells for what feels like the hundredth time. "Jojo, you are meeting the love of your life for a night of pure passion. Could you try to look pleased about it, sweetheart?"

My handsome co-star chuckles.

"You look a little too pleased for a man beginning to suspect his lover might be a psychopath, Blake," Harrison snaps. Blake gives me a discreet wink. We've worked together before. Blake is happily married with two kids, and Alex and I have had numerous lunches with him and his wife. I smile back, but both of us are far more somber as we get back to work.

Fenn is wilting on the drive home. She doesn't need to attend the set every day, but she always comes with me on the first day of filming, to check that every clause in my contract is being upheld.

"I'll see you tomorrow," she yawns when Phillip pulls up outside her house. Seb waves at us through the window and I wave back. I've always liked Fenn's boyfriend. He is unapologetically honest, and he adores Fenn.

It's well past midnight when I finally collapse into bed. I check my phone to find another message from Alex. *Goodnight, beautiful.* I pull my pillow over my head and sob until my chest aches.

When Alex arrives the following morning, I've composed myself. I've deliberately dressed down and left my hair loose, but I did apply a liberal amount of foundation to cover the angry red blotches on my face. That's what a night spent crying gets me.

I'm sitting at the kitchen counter, a cup of coffee in hand when he walks in. I don't lift my chin when he leans down to kiss me hello.

Ever perceptive, Alex picks up on it immediately. "What's wrong?"

I take a deep breath. "We need to talk."

He opens the refrigerator and pours himself some orange juice. "That sounds serious," he smiles.

"It is."

His smile falters, and I set down my cup.

"I need a break."

"What?"

"I know that sounds cheesy, but I've been doing a lot of thinking, and I just don't think I can handle us right now, not with everything else going on."

He's frozen in place, the still-open fridge sending a cool blast of air toward me. "Is this a joke?"

"No."

In an instant, he's at my side. "You can't be serious."

"I am. Very serious."

"Are you seeing someone else?"

Well, that escalated quickly. "No, of course not."

"Then what? You're not in love with me anymore?" I've never heard him sound so scathing.

"It's not that." I can't bring myself to say it. He knows me too well, he will see right through me.

"Then what is it?"

"I just... I need some time apart."

"Don't give me that bullshit! I'm leaving for South America in two days, you'll have ten days on your own. We barely see enough of each other as it is."

"I know. I'm sorry, I wish I could explain. I'm trying—"

He cuts across me, a whiplash. "Try harder."

"Alex, please. I just need some time to sort my head out."

"You're asking me for a *break*? What are we, seventeen?" He snatches up my hand and shoves it into my face until the five-carat diamond is all I can see.

"Ouch! Alex, you're hurting me."

"Good. Then you know how I feel. This is not a joke, Jojo. I proposed, you accepted. You don't get to just walk away from that."

I jerk my hand free and get to my feet. "I decide what I get to do," I snap. My hand tingles as the blood rushes back to my fingers. I rub at the red mark he left there. Alex catches sight of it, and all the fight goes out of him.

"Jesus, I'm sorry." He takes a step toward me, but I hold up both my hands, warding him off. I'm not afraid of him. I'm afraid of losing my resolve if he touches me, but Alex can't see that.

"I didn't mean to," he whispers.

"I know."

"You're making a mistake. You *know* you're making a mistake."

I swallow the lump in my throat and slide the ring from my finger. My hand feels naked without it. "Here."

"No." He shakes his head in denial. "Please don't do this. I'm leaving soon anyway. Take two weeks, get your head right. I won't contact you, and we can talk again when I'm back."

"I don't think that's going to happen." I'm dangerously close to losing it. I set the ring in his hand. "I'm sorry, Alex, but for now this is it. It's over."

On Saturday morning, without work to occupy my mind, I wander around the house in a depressed daze. I haven't heard from Alex. I hate myself for doing it, but on Wednesday I leaked a story to the press about our break up. I hate what this must be doing to him. For the thousandth time, I curse the day I started writing that book. I lied, that's the bottom line. After losing my virginity to Ace only to have him walk away without so much as a second glance, I wanted to forget it ever happened. I buried it and started fresh. He had taken something beautiful from me, so I had simply taken it back. I'd never told a single soul about Ace. Not even my roommate at the time had known. When I'd woken up in the morning to find Ace gone, I'd been gutted. I'd walked through the apartment looking for him. All I'd found was Casey, hungover and eating toast. She must have just got back; her hair was still wet from the shower.

At first, I thought maybe he'd just gone home for a change of clothes. It was probably best that Casey didn't see him. He'd been top of her hit list for a few months, and he'd rejected her on numerous occasions, which had only fuelled Casey's desire to have him. It was only when she told me that Ace was leaving for Paris that night that I realized I'd been played.

"You didn't know?" Casey had asked. "Where've you been all semester? He was offered a place in the theatre abroad program months ago. *Everybody* knew he was going."

BLINKING BACK TEARS OF ANGER, I fetch Noodle's leash from the hall.

"Let's go for a walk," I tell her. Noodle yaps in agreement.

I walk right into him in the lobby.

"I read about your break up," he says, "I'm sorry things didn't work out."

I grit my teeth and shove past him, but of course he follows me onto the street.

"Cute dog. What's her name?"

"Screw you."

"Interesting choice. I would've gone for something a little more fitting. Runt, maybe, or Street Rat."

Sensing my distress, Noodle growls at him. Ace drops to his knee and disarms her in five seconds flat. I watch his fingers kneading the tips of her pointed ears, and I feel a wave of hatred surge inside me.

"What do you want?"

"What do you mean? I'm here for our first date. I figured I wouldn't hold my breath waiting for your call." He stands and takes the lead from my hands. I jerk away as his free hand comes around my waist.

"What the hell do you think you're doing?"

"I'm giving them something to report." I don't know how he spotted the paparazzi, but he points directly at them. Two men in grey hoodies with long-range camera lenses pointed right at us.

"I only broke up with Alex four days ago," I hiss. "Can't we at least wait a few weeks?" All I can think of is Alex asking if I'd met someone else. I'd told him no.

"Sadly not," Ace says. His fingers brush the top of my buttocks as his hand returns to my waist. "Now, where are we off to? The park?" he gives a low whistle, and Noodle jumps on the spot. "Definitely the park," Ace laughs.

"I hate you."

He doesn't respond, only pulls me tighter against his side. He's enjoying this. I figure the paparazzi have enough photographs to last a lifetime by the time we make our way back home. My shoulders are aching with being tensed for so long, and my heart is in ribbons. Alex and I will never come back from this.

"What did you see in him, anyway?" Ace asks as if reading my thoughts.

"You mean other than the fact that he's handsome, successful, and the most considerate man on the planet?"

"You can't possibly know that for sure. Have you *met* every man on the planet?"

"You don't get to make jokes about it. This is my *life* we're talking about."

Frank narrows his eyes as we pass, but he doesn't say anything. My stomach curls as we ride the elevator up. Ursula doesn't work weekends, and the thought of being alone with Ace is terrifying. Who knows what he's capable of.

"What happened to you?" I ask abruptly. "You were voted most likely to succeed. You had the respect of every person in our class. You got into the abroad program, which is basically the fast-track to success. What happened?"

He meets my gaze. Something flickers in his blue eyes. "I had a change of heart. I dropped out after one semester."

"You stopped acting? Why?"

"I wanted to do something else. I was only in France for six months."

"What did you want to do?"

The elevator door opens, and his mask slips back into place.

"After you," he says, sweeping his arm out before him.

I snatch Noodle's leash and stomp to my door. "Before you get any ideas, you should know I studied martial arts for six months when I filmed *Heaven Rising*."

His cheek dimples. "Good to know."

As we move through my apartment, I can't help but see it through his eyes. Every luxury now feels like more motive for him to follow through with his revolting plan. To my surprise, he barely seems to notice his surroundings. Instead, he flops onto the cream couch in the living room and switches on the television.

"How long do you plan on staying?" I ask. "I have work to do."

His eyes don't leave the screen. "Go ahead, I'll be fine."

Noodle leaps onto the couch beside him and lays her head in his lap. I storm out of the room, but I can hear him chuckling all the way to my office.

Twenty minutes later, Ace sticks his head into the office. "Is something burning?" He catches sight of the flames coming from my bin and leaps into action. "What the fuck, Josie!" He scans the surface of my desk and grabs my water jug. The water douses the flames, leaving behind a haze of smoke and the acrid smell of burning paper.

"Are those your books?" Ace asks, peering into the bin. I smile sweetly, but my triumph is short-lived. Ace throws back his head and laughs.

"You burnt them? You think the truth is that easy to hide? There are hundreds of thousands of copies all across the globe. Besides," he adds, tapping a lean finger to his temple. "It's all up here, Jojo. Every sexy second of it."

"I wouldn't call your drunken fumbling sexy."

"Funny, because that's exactly what you called it that night." He raises the pitch of his voice and groans in a breathless whisper. "God, you're sexy. Don't stop, Ace. Please, don't stop."

All the blood rushes to my head as he repeats the words I moaned that night, almost verbatim. I gape at him, mortified. He taps his finger against his temple again. "All up here," he echoes.

I choke back a sob. "You're a bastard."

"And you're a spoilt brat."

My phone rings and we both jump. It's Alex. I can't answer it. I know exactly why he's calling. The rumor mill operates at lightning speed.

Tears well in my eyes. "Please leave," I beg. "I'll go through with this, but for now, please just go and leave me alone."

Ace walks forward and checks the screen on my phone. His face betrays not an ounce of sympathy when he reads Alex's name.

"You don't seem to understand how this works, princess," he tells me. "I live here now. I'm not going anywhere."

10

I spend the weekend hibernating in my bedroom and ignoring Alex's calls. I finally cave and listen to his voice mails. The fury and despair in his voice crucify me, but I don't call him back.

Ace has been quiet. I hear him moving around, but I don't see him again until Sunday evening when he barges into my bedroom without knocking.

"Get your ass out of that bed and into the shower. I've made soup, it'll be ready in ten minutes."

"I'm not hungry."

"I don't care. I've made it, and you'll eat it, even if I have to force feed it down your throat. God, Jojo, I never figured you for such a wuss."

"And I never figured you would turn out to be the world's biggest prick!"

He gives me an encouraging nod. "That's the spirit. Now get up. If you're not at the table in fifteen minutes, I'll be back to fetch you."

I take one look at the soup and push the plate aside. "I hate mushrooms."

"No, you don't. You love mushrooms."

"How would you know?"

"Because I watched you inhale a whole bowl after Hamlet."

It had been a first-year Julliard production. "You weren't even in Hamlet."

"No, but Kingman was. I spent a lot of time backstage with him."

"Do you still keep in contact with him?"

"I see him from time to time. He lives out in Vermont, teaches drama at his local college. Do you know he married Simone Wells? I think she played the clarinet."

I did know, but I'd never liked Simone. "Does Kingman know you've stooped to blackmailing women?"

"No. Although, considering his looks, I'm pretty sure he didn't land Simone the conventional way." Ace has a way of saying outrageous things in such a dead-pan manner I'm not sure when he's serious.

"Are you going to tell me why you quit acting?"

"I already did."

I shake my head and take a spoonful of soup. It's not bad.

"Where did you learn to cook?"

He gives me a wry look. "So you're speaking to me now?"

"I have staff, they'll be back tomorrow. I assume the sooner we get you in the spotlight, the sooner you'll be gone, so I guess it's in my best interest to make this performance believable."

"You see, that wasn't so hard, was it?"

There's a long silence while we eat.

"My mother taught me how to cook," he admits eventually. "She actually worked in a diner before she married my dad. She always wanted to have her own restaurant."

"Maybe when you're rich and famous you could set her up," I snap.

"She died, shortly after I left Julliard."

I wince. "I'm sorry."

"Why? It wasn't your fault."

"What happened?"

His face tightens. "She was in the wrong place at the wrong time."

I can tell from his expression that the subject is closed.

"And your dad?"

"He moved to the west coast shortly after it happened. He has a brother out there. They play bowls."

I open my mouth to ask him if his dad is any good but then decide against it. I don't want to know. Hearing him speak about his family only makes him seem more human, and I don't want to think of him as anything but the man intent on destroying my life.

"What about your parents?" Ace asks, seemingly oblivious to the turmoil waging war inside me. "Do they still live out in Connecticut?"

My spoon drops into the bowl with a clatter. "Enough. Stop acting as if we're so close you remember anything about me."

"But I do remember."

"Why?"

"Why do I remember you telling me your parents lived in Bridgeport?" he seems genuinely confused.

"No, why do you care?"

"I'm just making conversation."

I drop my chin to my chest and squeeze my eyes tightly shut. When I look up again, I've composed myself.

"I'm going to bed. I have to be on set early tomorrow."

Ace gets to his feet and stacks my bowl on top of his. "What time are we leaving?"

"I am leaving at seven. You're not coming with me."

"I am, actually. What better way for me to start rubbing shoulders with the who's who of Hollywood."

I scramble for an excuse. "It's a closed set."

"Uh-huh. Sure it is," he calls my bluff.

"Fine, it's not a closed set, but I can't have you wandering around getting in everyone's way."

"Don't worry, you won't even know I'm there."

WHEN I GET BACK to my room, my phone is ringing. I glance at the screen, bracing myself for the gut-twisting pain that plagues me every time I see Alex's name. Instead, a new terror comes over me. "Jojo!" CeeCee yells the second I answer. "I'm your fucking publicist, and I have to read about your break up on page two! What the hell is going on?" Knowing CeeCee, she's as upset about page two as she is about me not telling her, but the death of a politician this week trumped my life events.

"I'm sorry, CeeCee. Everything happened so suddenly, I didn't even think."

"Jojo, you know how this works. We issue a joint statement, we protect your image. We get on top of things before the rumor mill spins it out of our control. What we *don't* do, is get caught on camera with our new boyfriend only days after a break-up."

I wince. "I don't know what to say. I'm sorry."

"Sorry isn't going to help." A note of pity creeps into her voice. "The public will crucify you for this."

"What do I do?"

"We need to issue a statement, immediately. I'll call it through to the newsroom tonight. Ray Jenkins owes me a favor, I'll get him to print it in tomorrow afternoon's papers. And none of this page two bullshit, either. It won't fix things, but it will soften the blow. In the meantime, you break up with that Tom Hardy wannabe and get back together with Alex. The only thing the public likes more than a nasty break-up is a romantic reconciliation."

I take a deep breath. "I can't do that."

"I'm not asking you, Jojo."

"It's over between me and Alex."

"I don't care. You're an actress, Jojo, so act. Alex won't want any bad publicity either, not with the foreign investments he's raking in. He'll play along. Just ride it out a few more weeks and then we can stage a mutual separation. You still have deep respect for one another, you wish each other only the best, et cetera et cetera."

"CeeCee you're not listening. I can't do it. You're going to have to find another way."

"There is no other way!"

"You're the best publicist in Hollywood. You'll find one. Say whatever you need to, I give you full permission to quote me."

I hang up before she can respond. I know CeeCee. Her ego is her downfall. If I say she can find a way, she'll damned well find a way, and I pray that she does because it looks like I might lose my reputation and my career along with Alex after all.

I switch off my phone and crawl between the sheets. I can't believe that in such a short space of time my entire life has gone right down the shit chute.

On set the following day, Ace is true to his word. I've barely seen him and, so far, no one has complained about him being there. By midday, I've almost forgotten that he's here until one of the make -up artists touching up my face asks me if the gorgeous blond man over there is one of my co-stars. I follow the line of her gaze to find Ace engaged in conversation with my stunt double. As we watch, she laughs uproariously at something he's said.

"No," I tell her firmly, "he's not."

I wave away her attempt to re-apply my lipstick.

"I'll come back. I need something to eat."

Ace joins me at the food table. "You're doing well," he remarks idly. "I was watching you earlier. You've come a long way from Julliard."

I pile salad onto my plate, refusing to acknowledge the compliment.

"How much longer do you have to stay?"

"We only have to re-shoot one scene. Probably an hour or so."

"Right, well there's something I need to do, so I'll just see you at home."

The casual way he says the word sets my hackles arise, but I grit my teeth. "Fine."

"I thought maybe we could go out for dinner tonight."

"I'm really not up to it. It's been a long day." I wait for him to reply but he doesn't, and when I raise my eyes to look at him, there's a resolute expression on his face.

"I'll book a table for seven," he says.

Fenn walks in as he's walking out. We'd left before she arrived for work this morning so this is the first time she's laying eyes on Ace. I'm surprised she doesn't give herself whiplash with the way she cranes her neck over her shoulder as he passes by. There's a newspaper tucked under her arm.

"Fenn, what are you doing here?"

"I tried you on your cell, but you didn't pick up."

"I'm working," I remind her pointedly. I never have my phone switched on during filming.

"I know. You don't have access to email either, and I thought you might want to see this before you go outside." She hands me the paper.

I flip it open and clap a hand to my mouth. The headline is enormous, taking up almost the entire front page. *JOJO FOLLOWS HER HEART*! Below is a black and white photo taken of Ace and I walking away from my apartment, his arm around my waist. With an expert eye, I scan my own face in the image. I don't look unhappy. In fact, my expression as I look up into Ace's eyes is one I never want to see on my face again.

"How did I not know any of this?" Fenn asks. That's the problem with Fenn. She's an excellent assistant, but she's too shrewd for her own good.

I ignore her and scan the article. Holy hell. I am going to murder CeeCee. It reads like a cliched rom-com. College sweethearts forced apart by circumstances. According to the article, I'm quoted as being the happiest I've ever been, although I regret the pain I have caused Alex and hope that one day he can come to understand that I had to follow my heart. I reach for my phone, realize it's stowed in my dressing room and hold out my hand for Fenn's.

"I need to call CeeCee."

"Uh huh." The look she gives me is pure 'I told you so' but she hands it over.

I'm just scrolling for CeeCee's number when Harrison barks. "Should we start without you, Jojo?" Given that the scene we're about to film features me exclusively, I take it that's a rhetorical question.

"I'll just wait in your dressing room," Fenn whispers, before hurrying off. She's always been terrified of Harrison. I take a deep breath and remove the dressing gown I wear during breaks to protect my clothing. The make-up artist darts forward and touches up my lipstick. Five minutes later, the camera is rolling.

When Harrison calls it a wrap for the day, I heave a sigh of relief. I can tell he's not impressed with my performance, but considering the day I've had, I don't feel as guilty as I should. I re-read the article on the way to my dressing room.

Wordlessly, Fenn hands me my phone.

"Is it true?" she asks while I wait for CeeCee to answer.

"Parts of it."

"Hello, lovely." I hear CeeCee purr down the line, "I gather you've seen the papers."

"I have. What were you thinking? When I said you needed to come up with something, this is not what I had in mind."

"Well, seeing as you didn't tell me what you did have in mind, I had to be creative," she counters.

"You've made it sound like I've spent the last six years pining for Ace!"

"I've made you seem less like a cold-hearted bitch who broke Alex's heart for the first cockafella who crossed your path." By her tone, I suspect that's exactly what she thinks I've done.

"Ace and I weren't college sweethearts. Anyone who went to Julliard with us will vouch for that."

"You were there at the same time. It's enough. I'm more concerned about what happened after college, to be honest."

"What do you mean?"

"I used every single resource at my disposal, Jojo, and believe me, I have plenty. You know what I found out about John Logan between when he left Julliard for France and the present day?"

Despite myself, my curiosity is piqued. "What?"

"Nothing. Absolutely nothing. It's like he fell off the face of the earth. There's no record of him anywhere. No employment history, no credit record, not one single social media account."

"That's impossible."

"My point exactly. How well do you know this man, Jojo? And why, pray tell, would you throw everything away for someone you clearly haven't seen in years?"

"It's complicated."

There's a long silence. "Should I be worried? Are you in some kind of trouble?"

"No. No, it's nothing like that."

"Look, this article is damage control. Your reputation should recover. I just hope you know what you're doing."

I hang up and shove the phone in my purse.

"I'm not even going to ask," Fenn says.

"That's probably best," I reply wearily. "Could you get Phillip to drive around back? I really am not up to any interrogation from the press right now."

By the time I get home, even my bones are tired. I'm not sure this day could get any worse. Then the elevator doors open and I'm certain of it.

"What the actual fuck is going on, Josie?" Jude thunders. He's standing in the hall outside my door, his hair a tangled mess as if he's been running his hands through it for the past hour.

"Jude," I sigh. "What are you doing here?"

"I closed the pub for the first time in twelve years so I could come and talk some sense into my best friend."

"You didn't have to do that."

"Yes, I did." He holds up a copy of the paper. "What is this shit? You've left Alex? For some guy I've never even heard of?"

"Yes." I hold my head high. Jude will see right through me if I so much as hesitate.

"Why?"

"Why do you think?"

"You're going to try to tell me that you're in love with this person?"

"I am."

He laughs, but it's an ugly, derisive sound. "Bullshit."

"Why do you care, anyway? You don't even like Alex."

"I liked him well enough. You love him, which is good enough for me."

"Maybe I didn't love him as much as you thought."

"You're not that good an actress, Jojo." It's a low blow and, combined with my stage name, which Jude never uses, it's probably the cruelest thing he could say to me.

"You should go. If you think I'm going to let you come into my home and insult me, you obviously don't know me as well as you thought you did."

"I'm starting to wonder if I ever knew you at all."

I press my fingers to my temple, trying to ward off the dull ache which has settled there. "Jude, please. Can't you just be happy for me?"

"Look at me." I really don't want to do that, but I tear my eyes upward. Jude takes a step forward, then another, until he's standing right in front of me. "What's going on, Josie?"

My eyes prickle. "I can't tell you."

All the fight seems to drain out of him. His face pales. "I knew it. You're in trouble, aren't you?" My eyes are swimming, and vision blurs. "Let me help you, please. Tell me what's going on."

"Josie?"

Horrified, I whirl around to find Ace in my now open doorway. The concerned expression on his face is replaced by anger when Jude steps around me to confront him.

"What have you done to her, you son of a bitch?"

I grab his arm. "Jude, please don't!" He shrugs off my hand, his fists white-knuckled at his sides. "And who are you, exactly?" Ace drawls, stepping outside the apartment and closing the door behind him.

"Someone who isn't going to stand by while you take advantage of Josie."

Ace manages to look bored. "And who says I'm taking advantage of her?" His eyes flicker to mine, brow raised in warning.

"Whatever you think you're doing, it ends now," Jude says.

"I'm not doing anything. Other than taking my girlfriend out for dinner," Ace replies. "Are you ready?" he adds, "I've booked for eight. If we don't leave soon, we'll be late." Jude may as well have left the room, for all the attention Ace pays him.

"She's not going anywhere with you."

"You don't speak for her," Ace reminds him.

Jude snatches up my hands. "Josie, please. We can figure this out."

I smile up at him. Jude is my best friend, and I'm very likely about to lose him too. I try to convey how sorry I am with one look, and then I gently pull away from him.

"I just need to change," I tell Ace. "I'll be ready in ten minutes."

Jude's face crumples.

"You should go," I tell him firmly. "Thank you for looking out for me, but it's really not necessary."

"In future, maybe you should call before you visit," Ace adds darkly.

Jude snaps. He lunges for Ace, swinging his arm in a powerful right hook. Ace ducks easily, grabbing Jude's wrist as his face thunders overhead and using his momentum against him. I rush forward as Jude crashes to the floor.

"Jude!"

"Don't touch me!" he yells, pushing me away as I reach for him. He gets to his feet, and we stare at one another, neither speaking a word.

Ace clears his throat. "The clock is ticking, Josie," he says. Jude gives me one last disgusted look and then shoves past Ace and into the elevator. The second the doors close, I burst into tears.

"You're going to ruin your make up," is all Ace says.

12

"I'm not getting on that thing," I insist fifteen minutes later when Ace leads me to a black motorcycle in the underground lot. He hands me a black helmet with a neon orange lightning bolt emblazoned on the side.

"I don't want to spend the night being blinded by camera flashes," he says, "and no one will recognize you with this over your head."

"I thought the whole point is to get you on the front page," I retort. "Isn't that how this works?"

"I think we've made enough headlines for one day." He pulls the dark visor on his own helmet down.

I expected Ace to have booked at *The Palms* or any of the celebrity-favored eateries on restaurant row, but instead, we weave through traffic and head downtown. I cling to Ace's waist, terrified with every lurch of the powerful engine.

When we pull up outside a quaint and quiet bistro, I'm begrudgingly relieved.

"You have helmet hair," Ace tells me. Self-conscious, I run my fingers through my hair, trying to fluff it up. "Don't worry, no one here will notice."

We sit at a table set for two at the very back. Ace offers me the seat facing away from the other diners, and I accept it gratefully.

I order a glass of wine, Ace a chocolate shake. I raise my brow at that. "I'm driving," he says by way of explanation.

I clutch my glass, missing the weight of Alex's ring on my finger.

"So, tell me about Jude," Ace begins once we've ordered.

I shrug, not wanting to discuss Jude with him. "He used to be my boss. Now we're friends."

"Did you and he ever...?" I throw him a filthy look which makes him chuckle. "No, then. Did he and Alex get along?"

"Not particularly."

"He fought pretty hard for a man he doesn't particularly care for."

"He cares about *me*."

"Point taken. And I assume that you haven't told him about our little arrangement?"

"What do you think?"

"I think that you're sulking and it doesn't become you."

"I'm not sulking."

He refills my wine with a deft hand. "What are you going to have to eat?"

"I'm not hungry."

"Are we really going to do this again?"

"Fine." I take the briefest look at the menu. The meals are simple and moderately priced. "I'll have a salmon salad." We both know there is no salmon salad on the menu.

Ace leans back in his chair, exasperated. "Why do you have to make everything so difficult?"

"You expect me to make this easy for you?"

"I expect you to admit defeat graciously."

The waiter returns to take our order and Ace orders two portions of calamari with chipotle mayonnaise. I don't tell him that I haven't eaten mayonnaise since college. The camera is unforgiving, and I've spent the past few years on a perpetual diet.

We lapse into an awkward silence. Well, I find it awkward. Ace looks completely content, lounging in his chair like God's gift to Calvin Klein.

I take a slug of my wine.

"What have you been doing since you left France?" I ask. "For work, I mean."

His eyes are dark as they cut to mine. "A bit of this and a bit of that."

I hold his gaze, refusing to let it go. Ace grins at me.

"I joined the French Foreign Legion. I even have a tattoo on my ass to prove it."

"You are so full of shit."

He takes a sip of water. "Yeah," he admits, to my surprise. "I am."

"You're really not going to tell me?"

"What does it matter? You're determined to think lowly of me, so why should I bother correcting you?"

"It's hard not to think lowly of you when you're blackmailing me for fame and fortune."

"As opposed to Mr. Forbes List, who only wanted to make you happy, I suppose?" There's a venom to his tone that is completely out of character.

"Don't you dare compare yourself to Alex!" I hiss. "And besides, he's rich and famous all on his own, without any help from me."

"Agree to disagree." He eyes me over his glass. "How did you meet?"

The abrupt question takes me by surprise. I sit back, my fingers fiddling with my napkin. "We met through a mutual friend. He set us up on a blind date." Ace doesn't respond. "We've been together for two and a half years."

"You think you can really know someone in such a short space of time?"

"Yes."

He pulls a face.

"Haven't you ever been in love, Ace?"

"Once," he replies darkly. "It didn't work out."

"What happened?"

"What do they say in the movies..." he pretends to think about it, "oh yes. She just wasn't that into me."

I flash him a wicked smile. "Smart girl."

"She was."

By the time our food arrives, the wine has relaxed me, if only slightly. I move onto water, not wanting to fall off the back of his motorcycle on the way home. I manage only a few bites before I push my plate away. Ace frowns, but I ignore him.

"Tell me more about this girl who broke your heart."

He looks at me as if I've just grown two heads. "Are you serious?" he asks when he realizes I'm waiting for an answer.

"Yes. I want to know. Call it morbid curiosity, not that there's anything morbid about it. In fact, I want to send her a congratulatory card."

"And what would it say, this card?"

I think for a second, tapping my finger to my top lip. "It would say, To the Woman who broke Ace's heart. You are amazing. We should be friends."

"Well, there you go then. Mission accomplished."

Now it's my turn to look confused.

"You really are an idiot, Josie," Ace sighs, calling for the bill.

"You're not making any sense," I snap. The combination of wine and mayonnaise is curdling in my stomach.

"Jesus Christ!" Ace shakes his head in disbelief. "Let me spell it out for you, then. It was *you*, Josie."

I blink up at him, all the air driven from my lungs.

"I wouldn't get worked up about it," Ace adds spitefully, "it was a very long time ago, and I didn't know any better."

"You were in love with me? When?"

Ace rubs at his jaw. "I'm pretty sure around the same time we made love, although it's possible it started before then." He arches his brow cynically. "You really didn't know?"

My fragile hold on my temper snaps. "You left me," I remind him. "If you had such strong feelings, why did you scuttle out before the sun came up and leave for Paris without so much as a text?"

"What?"

"You heard me. Do you have any idea how mortifying it was to wake up to an empty bed? I cried for a month, you heartless bastard!"

"Josie..." he shakes his head, his eyes wide with shock. "I didn't leave you. I came back."

"No, you didn't."

"I did. I went to get you breakfast. But when I got back to your dorm, your roommate told me you'd gone out, and that you'd asked her to give me a message."

"What message?"

"That you didn't really want to deal with the whole morning after drama. I was leaving, and I'd considered changing my flight so we could work out what was happening between us, but she said you didn't want to see me again."

"She didn't. She couldn't have..." I rack my brain, trying to recall the details of that morning. Casey had been home when I came through from my bedroom. She hadn't said a word to me about Ace.

"Hold on a minute. Are you telling me that all this time you thought I just up and left after that night, without so much as a second thought?" he doesn't wait for my reply before he continues, his voice stricken. "Well shit. No wonder you think I'm an asshole."

"Casey had a thing for you," I whisper, remembering. Ace looks disgusted.

"I'm sorry," he says, sounding sincere for the first time since this all began. "I should've known better."

I swallow down the bitter lump in my throat and gather my wits. "Like you said, it was a long time ago."

"Really? You're just going to brush this off?"

"What do you expect me to do? You might not have been an asshole then, but you're blackmailing me now. This doesn't change anything."

Something fierce and furious flashes across his face. "What if I wasn't the bad guy in all of this?" he asks.

I think of Jude's stricken face earlier, and Alex's emotional texts. "But you are."

The ride home is hell. I do everything in my power to avoid touching any part of Ace's body, but it leaves me feeling vulnerable and terrified that I might fall. We are almost home when a car pulls out in front of us, and Ace swerves violently to avoid a collision. I scream, feeling my body tilting dangerously to the left. His arm shoots out to steady me, and I cling to it, chest heaving. The second we stop in the underground lot, he's off the bike, whipping off his helmet.

"Are you okay?" he asks, helping me unbuckle my own. I nod, and his fingers brush the hollow of my throat.

I step away as if he's burned me. "I can do it!"

Ace curses. He waits while I fumble with the clip. "You sure you're okay?" he asks again when I'm finally free of the stifling helmet.

"I said I'm fine!" I shove the helmet at him. "But I am never getting on that death trap again."

He follows me into the elevator. The space is too small, and I press myself into the opposite wall, trying to get as far from him as possible.

"Stop that," he snaps.

I ignore him. Ace's chest rises and falls with every breath. He's furious, and he keeps his hands glued to his side as if he doesn't quite know what to do with them.

"Screw it." In the same instant he rams his finger against the emergency stop button, he rounds on me, blue eyes flashing. His hands are warm against my cheeks as he seizes hold of my face and before I can register what's happening, his lips crush down on mine. He doesn't wait for me to yield. His tongue sweeps into my mouth, hard and merciless. My head swims. I press my hands to his chest, intending to push him away, but somehow, I am gripping the front of his shirt and pulling him closer instead. Warmth blazes in my belly, spreading like wildfire through my body. My tongue clashes against his, and I arch my body into his, feeling the hardness of him press into me. The sound that escapes from my throat is barely human.

When he suddenly pulls away, I am left clinging to him, limp and breathless. Reality crashes over me. Tears of shame well in my eyes.

Ace turns his back on me, his shoulders heaving. I cover my traitorous mouth with my hand. I can still feel his lips on mine, worse, I ache for them.

Ace reaches over and releases the emergency stop, and the elevator continues upward as if nothing's happened. As if my life didn't just veer off its axis. Ace doesn't look at me once as he leads the way to the apartment door, and, once inside, I rush straight to my room to soak Noodle's fur with my tears.

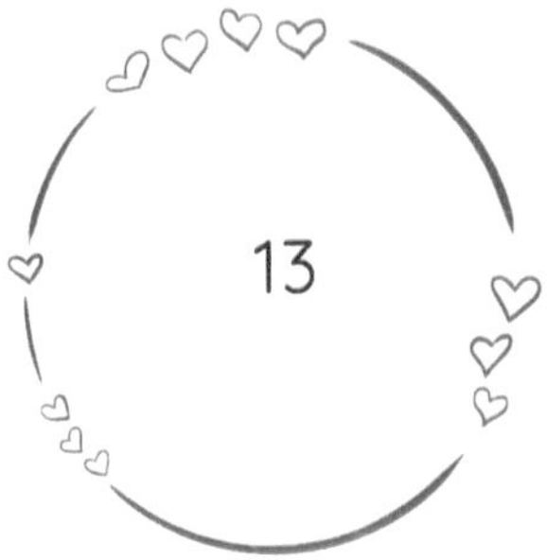

On Saturday, we take Noodle for a walk to the park. We've barely spoken since the kiss in the elevator, but that doesn't stop me reliving it over and over in my head. I kissed him back. After everything he's done, I threw myself at him. Every time I recall how I pressed myself against him, a deep blush shames my cheeks. I haven't heard from Jude, and my heart is heavy with his absence. I keep reminding myself that the only way out is through, and that the sooner Ace gets what he wants, the sooner he'll leave me alone. Maybe once all this is over, I can try to put the pieces of my life back together.

"Do you want a coffee?" Ace asks when I let Noodle off the lead. I nod, and he saunters off toward the mobile coffee cart. I take a seat on a dark green park bench and pick absent-mindedly at the peeling paint.

"Miss Hudson?" The man looming over me is dressed in blue jeans and a navy sweater. I don't like the look on his face. I've seen it once before, on an obsessed fan, and it ended with a restraining order.

I risk a glance at the coffee cart. Ace is in line, his broad shoulders towering over the girl behind him. "Can I help you?" I ask politely.

"I was wondering if I could get your autograph?"

"Sure. Do you have a pen?"

He shrugs, but the movement is too practiced, too obvious to be sincere. "I don't. Maybe we could go into that café over there and borrow one? I could buy you a coffee?"

I am not going anywhere with this man. "I'm sorry, I'm actually waiting for my boyfriend." I wave a casual hand toward the cart. The man's expression changes instantly.

"It's just a coffee," he says through gritted teeth.

"I'm really sorry, but I can't."

"Is this how you treat your fans?" he's dropping the act so fast I can barely keep up. "What, you think you're so high and mighty that you don't have a minute to spare for someone like me?"

I get to my feet. "I really think you should leave." Hearing the jangle of her lead, Noodle comes running.

"Is this your dog?" his eyes flicker. Before I can deny it, he's scooped her up. Noodle growls.

"Please put her down."

This time his smile is smug. "I will if you agree to that coffee."

"I'm not going to do that. Please put her down, or I'll call the cops."

He gives me a withering look and starts to walk off.

"Dammit!" I follow, throwing a desperate look over my shoulder. I can't see Ace anywhere. "Put her down!" I yell. I'm jogging now to keep up.

Realizing something is very, very wrong, Noodle starts to panic. I can see her tiny body squirming in his arms. *Please, God, don't drop her.*

"Put the dog down."

I've never been so relieved to see anyone in my life. Ace is standing a few yards away, blocking the path and cutting off the man's escape.

"And what if I say no."

"That would be your second mistake."

"Oh really?" A sneer. "And what was my first?"

"Forgetting that wherever Jojo goes, the press follows." He points toward the crowd of paparazzi that has gathered, their lenses trained on us.

"Please give her back," I say, sensing his growing agitation. He's got nowhere to go, and he knows it.

"You're a bitch," he hisses, shoving Noodle toward me. It's not the first time I've been called that, and it certainly won't be the last. I feel a rush of relief as Noodle leaps into my arms. "A filthy whore!" the man continues. Then he spits at me. Ace moves so fast it defies belief. In one rapid movement, he grabs hold of the man's hand and twists, jerking his body until he has his arm pinned at an unnatural angle behind his back. The man gives a yelp of pain.

"Apologise," Ace growls in his ear.

"Fuck you."

Another savage twist and I swear I hear muscle tearing.

"I'm sorry!" he howls.

"Let him go!" I yell at the same time. Ace does, but not before placing a well-timed kick in his arse, sending the man sprawling face-first onto the grass.

The click of the hovering cameras blurs into one long endless loop. I don't wait for Ace as I stalk off, but he appears beside me a second later, two coffees in hand.

"I shouldn't have left you alone," he says. It's the most apologetic I've ever heard him.

"It's fine. It happens all the time."

"How do you cope?"

I shrug. "It's part of the job."

SUNDAY'S HEADLINES must be exactly what Ace had imagined when he decided to blackmail me. The papers are all calling him a hero, one who saved me from the creepy stalker. I roll my eyes and toss them all in a heap on the couch.

"You can start a scrapbook," I tell him.

He barely looks up from the TV. "Nah, I'm okay."

He's wearing a pair of shorts and a T-shirt. My eyes linger on the powerful muscles in his thighs. I can see a faint line just above the hem, where his legs are a shade lighter than the rest of him.

"You see something you like, Josie?" I whip my head up to find him watching me, a teasing light in his eyes.

"You are so full of shit."

His eyes drift toward the Baby Grand. "Do you ever play anymore?"

"Not much."

"Why not?"

"No time."

He gives me an arch look and then swings his long legs off the couch. He's at the piano in three strides. I shake my head when he pats the small space on the stool next to him. His long fingers play a few test notes.

"It needs tuning," he announces cockily.

"It does not."

A few more chords and then he shrugs. I hold my breath as his fingers launch into action, playing a melodic ditty I've never heard before. He hits more than a dozen wrong notes, but he plays through them, not bothered.

"You're terrible," I say when he's done.

He grins. "Music was never my forte." Then, his face turning serious, "but I always thought it was yours. I thought this is what you'd be doing, in the end." He makes a sweeping motion over the keys to emphasize his point. "Not acting."

It's my turn to shrug. "Acting pays better."

"I'll take your word for it." He gets up and offers me the stool. "Why don't you play something now?"

I shake my head. "I'm going to get something to drink."

"Could you grab me a soda while you're there?"

"How positively domestic." We both jump at the new voice which cuts through the room.

"Alex!" I breathe. He's standing at the doorway to the living room, still wearing his traveling coat. He must have come straight from the airport.

"Hello, Jojo." His voice is pained, and dark circles shadow his eyes.

"What are you doing here?"

He stares at me, as if he's memorizing every inch of my face. "I don't know," he admits. "I thought you'd be alone."

"This is—"

"I know who he is."

Ace gets to his feet. Holds out his hand. "Nice to meet you... Alex, is it?"

Son of a bitch. It's a wicked move, as disrespectful as it is condescending.

Alex doesn't move a muscle and Ace lets his hand drop back to his side with a smug grin.

"Let's go into the kitchen," I say quickly, drawing Alex away from Ace. The second we're out of sight, Alex lowers his guard.

"What the fuck is going on, Jojo?" his voice is more venomous than I've ever heard it. "You end things with me, and a couple of days later this stranger moves into your house!"

"I know. It's a lot to take in, I get that. I don't know what to tell you—"

"Why don't you start by telling me exactly how long you've been seeing him?"

"I didn't leave you for Ace if that's what you're implying."

"Bullshit. What kind of a fool do you take me for?"

"I know it looks that way, but I swear to you, Alex, I wasn't seeing Ace before we broke up. We dated back in college, as you've probably read, and we bumped into each other at—"

"Your book launch. I know, I was there, remember?"

"Yes," I admit. "I'm sorry."

"Sorry?" he barks. "You've made me a laughing stock and all you can say is you're sorry?"

I've never seen him so out of control. He's always been so poised and perfect, and I hate that I am the cause of it. "I don't know what else to say."

"Are you sleeping with him?"

My mouth drops open. "No!" I exclaim, perfectly outraged, when all I can think is I'm so relieved he worded it like that and not 'have you slept with him'.

"Forgive me for assuming the worst," he snaps, "but it's hard to know what to think when your fiancé leaves you, and another man moves into her home a week later."

"He's sleeping in the spare room," I mumble. It's all I can give him. Alex slept in my bed every time he stayed over, and I hope that that means something, however small.

"Is that supposed to make me feel better?"

"No. In fact, I shouldn't be telling you any of this. We broke up, Alex. What I do with my time and who I spend it with, is no longer your concern."

He drags his hand across his face. "This is ridiculous. You don't just throw away two and half years for some deadbeat." At my look of surprise, his lips curve upward in a cruel smirk. "I did my research, Jojo. Your new boyfriend doesn't even have a job. He's obviously here for one reason."

"Oh really," I snap. He's absolutely right, but it still hurts to hear that he doesn't believe Ace could give a damn about me. "And what reason is that?"

"Your money, Jojo. In fact, I'll prove it." Before I can stop him, he strides out of the kitchen.

Ace is still lounging on the couch, but I can tell by his body language that he's not half as calm as he's pretending to be. He glances up as Alex enters, then shoots me a curious look.

"Logan is it?" Alex asks, and it's such a territorial thing to call Ace by his last name that I want to laugh, until Alex opens his mouth again. "Well, Logan, I have a proposition for you."

"You're not really my type," Ace drawls.

Alex's feigned laughter is grating. "I'll give you a million dollars to break up with Jojo."

I actually take a physical step backward. This isn't some romantic notion in a role I'm playing. This is my life. And Alex just put a literal price on my head.

"Are you for real?" Ace's voice is low, lower even than when he confronted the man in the park.

"You're obviously not here for any noble reason," Alex continues calmly, "so rather than waste all of our time, let's get to the point. A million dollars for you to walk away."

Ace gets to his feet. He's a full head taller than Alex. My feet are frozen in place, I couldn't move if I wanted to.

"A million dollars," Ace muses. His eyes meet mine over Alex's head. A storm is brewing. "What do you say, Josie?" Ace asks me, and his voice is so gentle I want to weep. "You think you're worth a million dollars?" His eyes pose a question, a challenge, and I rise to it beautifully.

"Alex," I say in a voice like honey, "get the fuck out of my house."

14

"I can't believe he offered me a million dollars," Ace muses, digging deep into the popcorn bowl for the burnt bits.

"I can't believe you turned it down."

He chuckles. "I think I could've pushed him for more."

"I think I could push you right down the stairs."

We're sitting on opposite ends of the couch. It took a full ten minutes for my heart rate to return to normal after Alex had left. Ace cocks his head to the side and fixes me in that intense stare of his.

"Can I ask you a question?"

"You just did."

"Why did you fall in love with him?" I arch my brow, and he holds up both hands in surrender. "I know, I know, he's perfect... God's gift to womankind and all that, but he just doesn't seem like someone you'd get involved with."

"How would you have any idea what kind of person I'd get involved with? You don't even know me."

"I know the girl you were. People don't change that much."

"I think you're proof that they do."

It's his turn to be silent.

"What happened, Ace? How did you go from being one of the nicest people in the world to this?"

"I wasn't that nice to begin with," he teases. "I did take advantage of you when you were drunk, remember?"

I blush crimson. I've become so used to denying it that any mention of that night turns me into a nervous wreck.

"Why did you lie?" he asks, "In the book, I mean. It would've sold no matter what you wrote, so why did you even say you were a virgin in the first place?"

"I guess I tried to forget it ever happened."

"Why?" his probing is gentle, but significant.

"You know why."

"Tell me."

"Because it hurt. I really thought... well, it doesn't matter what I thought. Once you left, I just wanted to forget it ever happened. I guess I considered myself a born-again virgin. It's very on trend at the moment," I add as his mouth falls open.

"Wait, so you haven't... I mean, since we...?"

I flush all the way down to my toes. "No, I haven't."

He whistles, low and loud. "Wow." His lip tugs upward. "And how did Mr. Forbes List feel about that?"

"I'm not discussing this with you. And wipe that smug smirk off your face."

I SPEND most of the following week on set, my emotions in chaos. Ace is a world-class prick, and yet I find myself enjoying his company. I even agreed to get back on his motorcycle after he called me out for being a wuss. And despite his claims that he wants to use me to further this own career, he hasn't done a single thing about it. Even Fenn is smitten. Once she got over her initial shock, she fell right under Ace's spell. She even offered to write up his resume and send it out on his behalf. Yesterday I overheard her telling him about a casting call downtown, and I had to take Noodle for an hour-long walk to calm down. George, of course, is thrilled, because with all the additional publicity I'm getting, the book sales have skyrocketed.

I have got to get out of this mess.

By Friday afternoon, I've started hatching a plan. I still haven't spoken to Jude but, as soon as filming ends, I make my way down to *The Office*.

"What are you doing here?" Jude asks when he sees me approaching the bar. It's happy hour, and a crowd of people fills the confined space. The only good thing about *The Office* is that the regulars have been around so long they knew me before I was famous, and they barely notice when I walk in.

"Can we speak, somewhere private?"

"As you can see, I'm a little busy."

"Fine." I slam open the hatch and move behind the bar.

"What the hell do you think you're doing?" Jude hisses.

"I'm freeing you up." I turn to the nearest crowd. "What'll it be?"

"Three beers, a scotch and soda, and a glass of red."

"You don't work here anymore, Josie."

"Don't worry," I say as I pull three beers from the cooler, "you don't have to pay me."

He curses under his breath. "Rachel!" a dark-haired girl taking a food order raises her head. "Cover for me, will you?"

The second she's behind the bar, Jude hauls me by my elbow to his tiny office down the hall.

"See, that wasn't so hard, was it?"

"I'm not in the mood, Josie."

I cave. "You were right. I'm in trouble."

He hesitates for only a fraction of a second before pointing to the chair behind his desk. "Sit."

Once he's perched on the desk before me, he instructs me to start from the beginning. So I do. His response is predictable as ever.

"Holy shit."

"I know."

"Why didn't you tell me. No, wait, don't answer that, I get why you didn't tell me. But why are you telling me now?"

"Because I have a plan."

"What is it?"

"George very clearly said that unless I'd slept with someone between getting engaged to Alex and writing the book, I was in the clear."

He pulls a face. "I really don't want to hear the specifics of your sex life, Josie."

"Bear with me. I was a 'virgin'," I put air quotes around the phrase, "when I wrote it."

"No, you weren't."

"I know, but you know what I mean. The point is, it doesn't really matter if I'm not a virgin after the fact."

"I literally have no idea where you're going with this. And please stop saying that word, it's freaking me out."

"I'm going to tell the world I had sex with Ace."

His expression is blank. "That's great, but I still don't get how it helps."

"I'm going to tell them I had sex with Ace *now*. That I'm not a virgin anymore. That way, I can control the story. If Ace tries to say we did it six years ago, no one will believe him, not after I make it front page news. It'd take the wind right out of his story. I'll be free."

"Okay, but you said he had photographs – evidence?"

"I haven't aged that much," I tease. "And they're not full-face photographs. He'd have a hard time proving when they were taken. I don't think he'd even bother, not when I've scooped his story. He'll run back to whatever hole he crawled out of, and I'd never have to see him again."

"Leaving you free to get back together with Alex?"

I hesitate. I hadn't even thought that far. In fact, Alex hadn't even crossed my mind.

Jude senses my distraction. "You *do* want to get back together with Alex, right?"

"Yes, of course I do."

"Don't sound so sure, you might hurt yourself."

"Alex offered Ace money," I blurt out. "To leave me."

"He *what*?"

"He came around, claimed that Ace was only in it for the money. He offered him a million dollars to walk away."

"Fuck me. What did Ace say?"

"He turned him down."

Jude steeples his fingers under his chin. "Why would he do that? A million dollars is a lot of money, and he wouldn't have to spend the next year of his life faking things with you."

"I have no idea. Who knows how Ace's brain works."

There's a pregnant pause, and then, "Alex really offered him money?"

"Yes."

"I never liked him."

I smile a small, sad smile. "I know."

Buoyed by the idea that I have a plan, I practically waltz home. The only downside is that for said plan to have any chance of success, I'm going to have to actually sleep with Ace.

As luck would have it, we're attending a premiere this weekend in Vegas, the original Sin City. We're catching an early flight tomorrow, so I spend the evening closeted in my bedroom, packing everything I might possibly need to stage my seduction. I'm absolutely terrified.

"What's wrong with you?" Ace asks when I get up from the table to wash up after dinner.

"What do you mean?"

"You haven't insulted me in at least thirty minutes. Something isn't right."

"Maybe I just want an evening of peace?"

"Lies. You're up to something."

I cast around for a change of subject. "Have you packed for tomorrow? You know you can use my name at any of the designer stores if you need something to wear."

"I'm fine, thanks."

"It's a premiere," I remind him, "you need to look the part."

"Are you worried I might embarrass you by showing up in jeans?"

"Yes."

"Ah," he teases, his eyes sparkling, "there she is."

In the greater scheme of things, his outfit is the least of my concerns, but I do find myself worried that he's going to embarrass me in front of the world's press.

On Saturday evening, having been primped and preened by a crew of hair and makeup artists, I wait with bated breath for Ace to emerge from his room. When he does, I almost fall over in my six-inch stilettos. I don't know where he got the suit, but it's perfectly tailored to show off the breadth of his shoulders and his long, lean legs. His shoes are leather – Italian, I'd bet my life on it – and his blond hair is slicked back, exposing the smooth tan of his forehead and his wicked blue eyes.

"Good enough for you, princess?" he asks arrogantly. He looks incredible, and he knows it.

I narrow my eyes. "Where did you get that suit?"

"I had it lying around. Shall we?" He offers me his arm, and I link my own through his. Once again, Ace blows me away with his performance. When we arrive at the Orleans Arena, he stands tall at my side, smiling expertly for the cameras, but not once does he step forward and command attention in the spotlight. I am hyper-aware of him, standing always at my back, guiding me through the reporters and foreign press. Watching the screening, I find I am analyzing every move I make, trying to see my performance through his eyes. It's not my favorite film, but I want him to like it. I don't know why I care.

Ace doesn't say much. At the after party, there are a few instances where he disappears and, despite scanning the crowd, I can't find him. I think I catch him talking to a serious man in a black suit who doesn't look as if he belongs here, but then one of my co-stars steps into my line of vision and I've lost him again. All in all, he's attentive and charming, but he falls silent the moment we get into the limo for the ride back to our hotel. My heart is hammering at a hundred beats a minute in anticipation of what I need to do, but Ace appears utterly relaxed, draped over the leather seat.

"You're very quiet," he remarks as we take the elevator up to the penthouse.

"I'm just tired. It's been a busy night."

He nods, but I don't think he believes me.

"I enjoyed the film."

"Really?"

"Really." He chuckles. "Don't look so surprised, I've always said you were a good actress."

"You could've been a brilliant actor," I remind him, "if you didn't quit."

His lips press together in a grim line. "I guess it wasn't meant to be."

It all comes crashing back – the real reason that he's here, the blackmail, and I bite my lip to keep from snapping at him. "I guess not."

The lights are turned low inside the apartment. "I'm going to take a shower," Ace says with a yawn. "You need anything before I go?"

"No, I'm fine."

I wait until I hear the hiss of the shower in his private bathroom, and then I hurtle through to my own room. I turn the taps on full, letting the cold water pour over me. *You can do this*, I tell myself over and over in my head. *You've done it before, it's not a big deal.*

The smooth satin slithers over my skin. Pale cream, it stops a good three inches above my knees and is low-cut enough that only a thin strip of lace protects my modesty. The matching scrap of underwear is so small I wonder why it was even included. I leave my hair loose and take off all trace of the heavy make up that caked my skin. Barefoot, I walk slowly back to the kitchen.

Ace has a habit of taking a bottle of water to bed with him every night. It's only a matter of time before he pads into the kitchen, wearing only a pair of sleeping shorts. He stops dead when he catches sight of me.

"I thought you said you didn't need anything."

I hold up a bottle of Evian. "I was thirsty."

"That's an interesting choice of nightwear."

I glance down at my lack of an outfit and shrug as if I barely noticed what I'd thrown on.

Ace doesn't buy it for a second. "What are you doing, Josie?"

Screw it. I set down the water and cross the room to stand right in front of him. With his height, I know he can see right down my negligee to the scrap of lace beneath. I hear his shocked intake of breath, and my lips curve upward in a small smile. "What does it look like I'm doing?"

"It looks like you're trying to seduce me." His voice is ragged, and it sends a bolt of heat through my chest.

"Is it working?"

He squirms uncomfortably. "That depends."

"On what?"

"On why?"

I tug my bottom lip between my teeth. "Maybe I'm tired of waiting for you to make the first move. You can't pretend you haven't felt something between us these past few weeks."

"You should go to bed."

I inch closer until only a hair's breadth separates us. The smell of him wafts over me – expensive soap and the musky smell of him beneath. His body is rigid, his jaw tics. He's using every ounce of restraint not to close the distance between us. I notice a small silver scar near his shoulder, another just above his left hip.

"Don't you want me, Ace?"

He doesn't move. I lift my hand and run my nail down his chest, from collarbone to the dark hair below his navel. A small shudder runs through him.

"I don't like games, Josie."

"I don't believe that." I rise onto my toes and brush my lips across his, featherlight. "You've been playing one since you came to see me at that book launch." Another kiss, but this time I let my tongue follow my lips. "I'm only trying to even the score."

There's one part of his body that he cannot control, and it rises up to meet me. The touch of it sends an electric shock through my thighs. Ace is undone. His lips crash onto mine, his fingers knot through my hair. I gasp against his mouth, reaching for him, caressing him through the soft cotton of his pants. Ace groans, his tongue meeting mine in a frantic clash of wills. When he lifts me up, my negligee rises to my waist, and I yelp as my bare arse meets the cold marble of the kitchen counter. He pulls the shoestring straps down my arms, as his mouth trails my jaw, my neck, and then closes over one of my breasts. I curse in agony and ecstasy as he moves away, burrowing my fingers into his hair, and pulling him back to my chest.

His fingers dip lower, and my whole body stiffens in anticipation. When he brushes over my panties, it burns, a deep throb that sends me over the edge. I bite down on his shoulder, my hands fumbling for his pants.

"Josie," he growls, his breath hot in my ear.

"Yes!" I pant in encouragement, my body arching toward his teasing fingers. Only his arm prevents me from falling as I teeter on the very edge of the counter, my legs falling wide. He peels off my panties with one steady hand and then lifts me toward him. I wrap my legs so tightly around his waist that I don't know if I'll ever unravel them again. When he lowers me onto the couch, he stands back to admire my naked body. I close my eyes and reach for him.

"Josie," he repeats. His voice has changed. I open my eyes to find the wicked grin firmly in place. "What are you doing?" I ask, suddenly terrified.

He gives my body one last lingering look and then leans forward until our noses are almost touching. His eyes loom in my vision.

"This is not a game," he says. He straightens up, fetches my abandoned water bottle from the kitchen counter, and disappears out the door.

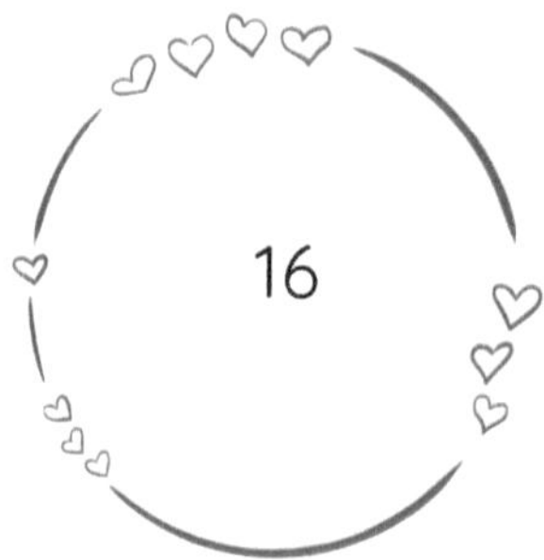

I spend the night cringing in despair. Not only did I fail, but Ace's rejection hurt far more than I expected. It's like that morning in college all over again. I don't cry. I refuse. This is my fault, because, as much as I convinced myself that my plan was all about escaping Ace, I'd wanted him. I'd completely let myself go last night. Even now, my body aches for him.

When the first light of dawn starts to filter through my window, I change my flight without telling Ace and catch a cab to the airport.

I don't go home. I send my bags with Phillip and spend the morning wandering through the park. I eat at the diner, the one place no one will look for me. When Ace calls, I don't answer. By the time his name shows up for the eighth time, I switch my phone to silent. Eventually, I'll have to go home and face him. I know I will, but I don't want to.

He's standing in the hall when I get home. His hair is disheveled, and a five o'clock shadow darkens his jaw. His expression is unreadable.

"Where have you been?"

"Out."

"Dammit, Josie!" He plunges his hands through his hair. "You can't just take off like that."

"I can do whatever I damned well please."

"This is about last night," he begins, but I shove past him, not letting him finish. I've just slammed my bedroom door when it bursts open. "Don't walk away from me."

"Get out."

"We need to talk about this."

"Get out!"

"No!"

I snatch up the lamp beside my bed and hurl it at him. He ducks easily, and it smashes into the wall behind him.

"Get the fuck out of my room!"

"You're behaving like a child!"

A book follows the lamp.

"That's enough!" Ace roars. He crosses the distance between us and seizes my hand before I can find my next weapon.

"Let me go!"

"Not until you've calmed down!" His face is so close to mine that I can make out flecks of green in the blue. My legs go out beneath me as my face crumples. Ace catches me as I fall. Heaving sobs wrack my body as I collapse against him, releasing all the pain and rejection I've been feeling since last night.

"Oh Jesus, Josie, I'm sorry." His arms tighten around me.

"You're not sorry," I cry, beating my hand against his chest. "You don't care, stop acting like you do!"

His voice is pained as he whispers against my hair. "But I do care."

"Stop it!" I plead. "Please stop it. I can't do this anymore."

"Why are you so upset?" His eyes are searching my face. "It was only a game."

I bite back another sob and shake my head.

"Josie." Firmer now. "It *was* only a game?" He's watching me closely. Something flashes in his eyes – triumph?

"It wasn't a game?" He's smiling now, and he's so beautiful it breaks my heart. "Josie, please, tell me. It wasn't a game?"

I squeeze my eyes together and shake my head again. Tenderly, he sets me down on the edge of my bed.

"Look at me."

I open my eyes.

"You're upset because I rejected you?" He sounds thrilled, and it drives home just how cruel he is.

"Please leave me alone," I whimper.

"No. You need to understand."

"Understand what, Ace?" I'm so tired, so very tired.

"I don't want to be a game to you. I thought... I never suspected..." he stops. Takes a deep breath. "Josie, I wanted you last night more than I've ever wanted any woman in my life. Except maybe you, six years ago." He wipes the tears from my eyes.

"But you left? You left me... naked," I add, and fresh tears spring to my eyes at the memory. "On the couch."

His teeth flash. "That was the hardest thing I've ever had to do in my life. Even after four cold showers, I'm pretty sure I've sustained a permanent injury."

I try not to smile and fail spectacularly. "You better not be screwing with me."

His face is the sun, blazing and triumphant. "Josie. There's nothing I'd rather be doing than screwing you."

This time, when he kisses me, there is none of the urgent frenzy of before. Instead, his kiss is tentative. I can feel him holding his breath, waiting for my silent approval. I lift my tear-stained face, allowing him easier access to my mouth, and he smiles against my lips. I part my own and slip my tongue into his mouth. Slowly, I explore every warm inch of it and Ace returns the favor. I close my eyes with a soft sigh, and he kisses my eyelids, tasting my tears.

His hands stroke my neck, my back, my thighs, sending tiny electric sparks along my skin. When his hands grip my shoulders and press me gently down, I lie back. He pulls off his shirt, giving me only a brief look at his muscular torso before his body covers mine. Every inch of him touches me. I feel light-headed, drugged, wrapped tightly in his arms.

We kiss, on and on, until my lips are swollen and sensitive. Until I think I might faint with desire.

Ace leans back, taking his full weight on his elbows, and I splay my hands on his chest. I trace the silvery scar with one finger.

"What happened?" I ask, my voice barely recognizable. He silences me with another lingering kiss. I already know every inch of his mouth, and I duck my head, letting my lips trace the strong line of his jaw. I breathe into his ear, and he stiffens. My hands move lower. This time, he lets me.

I WAKE up draped across Ace's bare chest. He's sleeping, the rise and fall of his chest marking every slow and steady breath. I trace the circular scar, feeling the twisted tissue, and then lift my head to check the matching scar near his hip. There's a long, thin scar in the groove of his collar bone, and another just left of his navel. I move my hand to touch it, but Ace's hand closes over mine. I look up into a pair of lazy blue eyes.

"What happened to you, Ace?" I ask.

"It's a long story."

"I'm not going anywhere," I say, but it's already too late. He's moved, twisting sideways to scoop me against him, his mouth meeting mine and I'm powerless to resist him.

When I finally drift back to earth, I bring it up again.

"Where did you get these scars?"

Ace sighs, realizing I am not going to drop it.

"I can't tell you."

I sit straight up in bed.

"What?" Somewhere in my addled brain, it registers that I thought this changed everything. That somehow after being intimate, all the walls would come down. Apparently, I was wrong.

Sensing that I'm about to bolt, Ace slides his arm around my waist, pinning me against him.

"Josie, I need you to trust me."

"How can I trust you if you won't be honest with me? What is going on? I know you're not here for fame, you've shown absolutely no interest in anything but me since you arrived."

"Can't you just believe that I want to be here and let it rest?"

"I need answers."

"I know. I just can't give them to you. Not yet, anyway."

"When, then?"

"I can't say. Soon."

I shrug out of his arms and scoot to the edge of the bed, as far as I can possibly get from him. "That's not good enough."

"Josie, please."

"I need something." I send up a silent prayer that he listens, because it's the truth. If Ace doesn't stop giving me secrets and lies, I have no choice but to end this. No matter how badly it crucifies me to do it.

"I can't," he says.

"Oh my God, Josie, what have you done?" CeeCee shrieks down the receiver.

"I told the truth."

"You can't do this! It doesn't work this way – you don't just go rogue on your publicist!"

I pick up the copy of *The Daily* which was delivered this morning. JOJO LOSES IT, the headline reads. The article is carefully worded, I know because I drafted it myself and sent it through to the newsroom yesterday. The accompanying photograph is one taken of Ace and I at the premiere. I'm smiling at the camera, and he's smiling down at me.

"I think I already have," I say, slamming the paper face down on my desk.

"Why? Why break *this*, of all stories?"

"It's the truth. I didn't want there to be any confusion."

"Christ Jojo, you lost your virginity. It's not something the entire world needs to know."

If only she were right. Sadly, this is the only way to get Ace out of my life. I haven't spoken to him since we made love two days ago. I'd left for work before dawn and stayed late on set both nights. He'd been asleep by the time I came home.

Tonight, I'd come home early, prepared to make my last stand, but he'd been out when I arrived. I pass the hours watching re-runs of old Hollywood movies and scratching Noodle's belly. When the front door slams with unnecessary force, I smile to myself.

"What the fuck have you done?" Ace is shaking with rage.

I stretch, deposit Noodle on the couch beside me and get to my feet. "Taking my life back. I've taken the liberty of packing your things," I add, gesturing at the Louis Vuitton luggage case beside the couch. "You can keep the bag, I have another."

"Dammit, Josie, this is serious."

"As am I. I want you out of my house. Right now, or I'll call the cops."

"You're bluffing."

I reach for my phone. Every muscle in my face is perfectly relaxed, displaying not a flicker of emotion.

"Don't do this."

"It's done, Ace. Get out."

"You have no idea what's going on. There's a bigger picture here, Josie."

"If I have no idea what's going on, it's no fault of mine," I reply pointedly. "And seeing that this," I lift the paper and wave it in his face, "leaves you with no bargaining chip, there's really nothing left to say."

"I won't leave you."

"Fine," I sigh. "We'll do this the hard way." I lift my phone and dial 911. I've barely hit the call button when Ace snatches my phone from my hand.

"Fine. I'll go, but this isn't over. I'll be back."

"No, Ace. You won't."

He leaves the bag. Granted, it only has a few of his clothes and a small toiletry bag, but still, I can't bear to have it in the apartment. I drag it downstairs and leave it beside Frank's station. When Fenn arrives bright and early the following morning, I ask her to make sure it's donated to charity.

I don't call Alex. For so long, all I could think of was getting back together with him, but now that I'm free to, I can't bring myself to do it. My only regret in running the article is the pain it must have caused him. A week passes, and I haven't heard a word from Ace. I throw myself into work. Filming will come to an end in a few days, and then we reconvene to shoot in Chicago in a few weeks. When I'm not at work, I spend hours at the Baby Grand. I haven't played like this in years, all raw emotion and vulnerability. Without any witnesses, I soak the ivory keys in tears.

The press is relentless. Noticing that Ace has been conspicuously absent, they are baying for blood. Cruel captions such as ONE NIGHT STAND? and WHAT A WASTE! dominate the headlines, but I pay them no heed. This will all blow over.

Avoiding the world's press, however, is far easier than avoiding my own family. Teddy arrives without warning ten days after I kicked Ace out. I find her waiting outside my door after the last day of filming.

"Sorry it took so long," she says. "I had to find a locum to fill in at the practice."

"Did mom and dad send you?" I ask.

She swipes a stray blonde tendril out of her eyes. "You bet your ass they did. And you should thank your lucky stars it's only me. It took me two whole days to convince dad not to get on a plane and come out here."

"I tried to call him to explain, but he wouldn't take my call."

"He's hopping mad." Teddy gives me a sympathetic look. "I'm assuming you have a good reason for all this crazy behavior?"

"You have no idea."

She scratches in her overnight bag and pulls out a bottle of wine. "Why don't you start at the beginning."

Teddy is my sister, and she loves me unconditionally. She also has the added benefit of having known me throughout my college life, and she clearly remembers the thumping crush I had on Ace.

"He just doesn't strike me as someone to do something like this," she says.

"I know. That's what makes it so weird."

"And he didn't offer any explanation. Or even a clue as to why he's being like this?"

I shake my head. "If he had, I wouldn't have kicked him out. Is dad really furious?"

"Josie, your cherry pop has been all over the news. What do you think?"

I bury my face in the couch cushion. "Oh, God."

"Yeah." She refills my glass. "And now you're not even together anymore, which isn't helping matters."

"You understand why I had to do it?"

"*I* do, but unfortunately no one else will. What really concerns me is that you don't look remotely pleased that your evil plan worked."

We've moved on to our second bottle when Jude arrives. It's his third visit since Ace left. He must be seriously worried about me to leave the bar so often. The sight of Teddy completely unnerves him.

"I didn't mean to interrupt—" he begins hesitantly.

"Oh, just come in," I snap.

He gives Teddy a look that is both apologetic and appreciative at once. "I need to speak to you," he tells me.

"About what?"

"Ace."

"Anything you say to me, you can say in front of Teddy. She knows everything."

He picks up my glass and takes a huge swig of wine. "I take it your plan backfired."

"My plan worked perfectly."

"Epic fail," Teddy counters with a small burp. Jude grins. "She's utterly in love with the handsome bastard."

"I knew it." Jude toasts her with my glass.

"Hey!" I snatch back the glass. "I'm sitting right here!"

"Pining," Teddy says.

"Miserable," Jude agrees.

"Why don't you just call him?" Teddy asks. "I'd like to meet him."

"You're pissed," I remind her. "You've forgotten that he's a liar."

"Oh, yes. He is a liar." Teddy gives me a narrow-eyed stare as if I'm playing Ace and she's practicing for when they meet.

"Don't waste it," I tell her solemnly. She straightens her face.

Jude fetches a glass, and we spend the evening curled on the couch. My head is on Jude's shoulder and, through squinted eyes, I see Teddy's feet in his lap. There are three empty bottles on the table.

"You know what I think would be a good idea?" I slur, after an extended silence.

"What?" Teddy yawns.

"You two should get married."

"Sure." Jude shrugs. "Why not."

"It's not like I have anything better to do," Teddy says.

"I can do it!"

Jude chuckles. "Not to take away from your impressive skill set, Josie, but I'm pretty sure it doesn't include marriage officiate."

"I'll be right back." I trip over my discarded shoes and bang my knee on the coffee table, but it doesn't deter me. Two minutes later I'm back, with my MacBook in hand.

"What are you doing?" Teddy grumbles. "I thought we were having a wedding."

"We are." A quick Google search and I hit pay dirt. "Ha! I knew it! I can get ordained in a couple of minutes."

Jude peers over my shoulder. "It can't be that easy."

"It is." I scroll down. "Some states require government registration, but California isn't one of them." I punch in my details and wait. Five minutes later, I'm ordained.

"Done." I grin at both of them. Then my eyes fall on Teddy's messy hair and her faded jeans and sweater combo. I frown. “Are you wearing that?”

She drops her chin to assess. “No. I’m going to raid your closet.”

“Go wild. I’m just going to download one of these sample ceremony scripts.”

Jude watches over my shoulder as I scan the different versions I could use.

“That one,” he says, jabbing at the screen.

“Minimalist?” I ask, squinting at the tiny text. “Are you worried I might forget my lines?” We both find that hilarious. Trying to compose himself, Jude sets down his glass.

“I better get neatened up too.” He’s wearing a checked shirt over a white Tee, and black jeans.

“How exactly are you going to neaten up?”

He does up all his buttons with clumsy hands. “Tah dah!”

“Completely transformed,” I giggle.

Jude laughs too, until Teddy steps back into the room. She looks exquisite in a dusty pink silk dress that I wore to the Golden Globes last year. She’s left her hair braided, and is barefoot, but her cheeks are rosy and her lips shimmer.

“Gorgeous!” I announce, clapping my hands in excitement. “Now, what are we going to use for rings?”

We’ve run out of wine, so Jude pours us all a whiskey while we try to figure it out.

“I’ve got it!” Teddy announces after I’ve tried and failed to stuff Jude’s man-sized ring finger into every piece of jewelery I own. “Tattoos.”

“Tattoos?”

“Yeah. A friend of mine did it, it’s awesome.”

“There’s a 24-hour tattoo parlor behind the bar,” Jude offers helpfully.

“Perfect!”

The ceremony is short and sweet. I take my role very seriously and adopt a solemn expression as I recite the vows that they repeat after me. When it comes to the "with this ring" part, I skip ahead to "I take you," and both Teddy and Jude say, "I do."

There's a tense moment when I ask if anyone present knows of any reason why these two should not be joined in matrimony. All three of us look around my living room as if, at any moment, a guest might jump up and object. Nothing happens. Noodle doesn't even stir in her sleep.

"Then by the power vested in me by the American Marriage Ministry and the state of California, I now pronounce you man and wife!" I announce grandly.

I've forgotten something. I glance down at my phone, where I've stored the script. Jude clears his throat. I glance up to find him jerking his head toward Teddy.

"Oh yes! You may kiss the bride!"

Jude doesn't need to be told twice. He dips Teddy and plants a kiss right on her mouth. It goes on a lot longer than I expected and when he's done, her lipstick is smeared, but her eyes are sparkling.

I manage to unearth a bottle of champagne from the bowels of my fridge before we pile into a taxi and head for *The Office*.

"Are you sure you want to do this?" I ask when we enter the tattoo parlor. It's dark, and a little seedy, but the guy who greets us from behind the counter seems pleasant enough.

"Hey, Aaron!" Jude tries to give him a high five but just misses.

"What's up, Jude? You finally in the market for some ink?"

"Actually, yes." Jude steers Teddy forward proudly. "This is Teddy. My *wife*."

"Awwwwww," I croon as Teddy blushes to the roots of her hair.

"Congrats man!" Aaron pumps Jude's hand. "It's a pleasure to meet you, Teddy. So, what are you wanting?"

"Rings."

"Nice. I get that a lot. You want any initials, or just a band?"

Jude and Teddy exchange looks. "Just a band, I think," Teddy says.

Aaron gives Jude a quick once over. "You're not intoxicated, are you?"

"I know what I'm doing if that's what you're getting at."

"It's not just that," Aaron says. "Besides making a permanent bad decision, there could be other implications – excessive bleeding, for example."

"Will we die?" Teddy asks, winking at Jude.

Aaron laughs. 'no."

"We're not drunk," Jude lies. He holds Aaron's gaze, refusing to back down.

"Okay." Aaron seems satisfied, "but you're going to have to sign these consent forms."

I wander around while Aaron gets to work and flip idly through the heavy sketchbooks on every conceivable surface.

"Are these your designs?" I ask, holding up a thick book bound in black leather. Aaron takes a minute to finish what he's doing before looking up.

"Yeah, those are mine."

"They're really good."

Jude is almost done. Teddy looks a little green. Teddy is a vet, but she's never liked needles. Jude's touch does what the champagne couldn't. Only when he takes her free hand in his, does Teddy relax. The way he looks down at her makes my heart want to jump out of my chest.

"All done," Aaron announces after applying a liberal smear of ointment around Teddy's finger. He removes his gloves and moves over to the counter.

"It's on me," I insist, handing over my card. Jude starts to argue, but I cut him a warning look. "Maid of honor privileges."

"Technically, you're also my best man."

"Exactly. This is my wedding gift to both of you."

We walk over to *The Office* for the after party. Laurel has been holding down the fort, but Jude quickly joins her behind the bar. As busy as he is, he makes sure that mine and Teddy's drinks are permanently filled. Laurel looks utterly crushed.

By the time the last patrons leave, I'm wilting on my stool. Teddy is dancing on her own between tables. Every now and again she stops to admire her new tattoo or blow a kiss at Jude.

We head back to my place around two a.m. I don't even have the energy to find pajamas. Instead, I drop my clothes at the foot of my bed and collapse onto the cotton sheets.

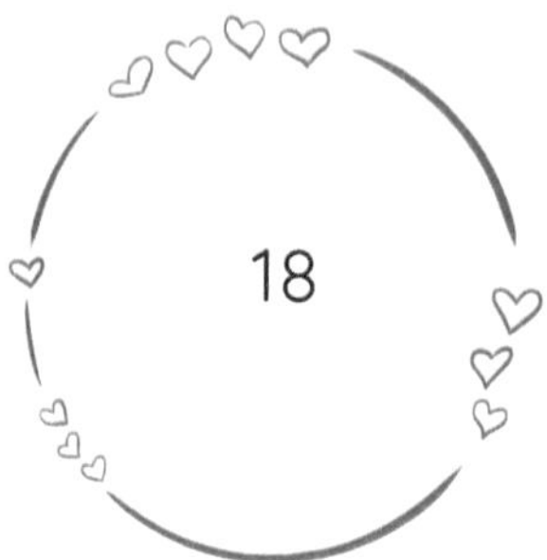

18

I wake with a dry mouth and a pounding headache. Wandering into the kitchen in only my gown, searching for Tylenol, I catch a glimpse of a bare ankle peeking over the edge of my couch. Curious, I round the corner and clap both hands over my eyes.

"Oh my God!"

Teddy sits bolt upright with a shriek of alarm, the sudden movement knocking Jude right off the couch. They're both stark naked.

I keep my eyes covered amidst the chaos of giggling while they search for their clothes.

"You can look now," Teddy tells me eventually. I drop my hand to find them both curled on the couch. Teddy is wearing Jude's checked shirt. Jude's white T-shirt is inside out. There's an empty champagne bottle on the floor.

Slowly, I piece together the fragments of last night. Teddy yawns, and as she covers her mouth with her hand, realization hits.

"Oh my God, Teddy!" I point at her finger, where the black band is visible through the clear dressing.

Teddy moves her hand away from her mouth and blinks at the

tattoo. Then her eyes cut to Jude's hand. Jude is staring at his own finger as if he's never seen it before.

"We got married," Teddy says.

"You got married," I confirm.

"We can't be married," Jude says. "There's no way Josie got ordained for real."

"Of course not," Teddy agrees quickly. Then she swallows. "Although, I'm more concerned about this right now!" she shoves her tattooed finger into his face as if he wielded the needle that put it there.

My MacBook is still open on the website I found last night. I scan it with Teddy breathing over my shoulder while Jude stumbles around in the kitchen making coffee.

"Okay, it says that I have a legal responsibility to complete a marriage certificate on the wedding day. We didn't do that, right?"

Jude sets down the mugs, and our eyes fall on the crumpled piece of paper below them. I recognize Teddy's signature at the bottom and Jude's jagged scrawl.

"That can't be legit," Teddy says.

"Look, it's going to be fine. I'll call them right now. Even if it turns out that this is official, we can just have the marriage annulled, right?"

"On what grounds?"

I rack my brain and then side eye Teddy. "You didn't consummate the marriage, did you?"

"We did," Jude answers easily. "Twice."

Teddy is dying. I try to keep a straight face, but I can't. "I'm throwing this couch out," I say. Jude starts to laugh.

"It isn't funny!" Teddy groans. "What are we going to do if we can't get this annulled?"

"It might not even be legal, Teddy."

"I have something to say," Jude interrupts. Teddy looks up at him, renewed hope flaring in her eyes. Jude, however, is frowning and I suspect what he's about to say isn't what Teddy is expecting.

"What if I don't want to have it annulled?"

It takes Teddy a moment to process. "What?"

Jude stares her down. "Yes, we were drunk, but that doesn't mean I didn't want to marry you."

"It's true," I concede. "Jude's loved you since," I try to come up with a date and settle for "well, since forever."

"He has not!"

"Actually," Jude says, without a trace of embarrassment, "I have."

Despite my hangover, I can't help but smirk. Teddy doesn't seem to know what to do with her face.

"That's... you're...," she sputters helplessly. She takes a deep breath and starts over. "You can't possibly expect this to work. We live on opposite sides of the country!"

"I'll move."

"What?"

"WHAT?" I echo Teddy's question. The thought of Jude leaving L.A is inconceivable, but his face is deadly serious.

"You'd move almost three thousand miles just to see if this might work?" Teddy asks.

"That's crazy," I snap. "Your whole life is here. What about *The Office*? You've spent years working to build something here and now that you have it, you're just going to up and leave?"

"I can find someone to manage the bar without me. Laurel's been there long enough, and she deserves a raise. I might even make her partner."

"But..."

Jude gives me a sad look. "You're right, Josie. I *have* spent years working. And do you know where it's got me? I'm thirty-four years old, and I haven't ever had a real relationship. Christ, I haven't even had a vacation in ten years." His gaze shifts from my face to Teddy's and his eyes soften. "Your sister is right. I've loved you since the first moment I saw you. So how about it, Teddy? I'd like permission from my wife, to date her."

I CAN'T BELIEVE I have to fly to Chicago this week. Teddy has extended her stay for a few days while she and Jude work this out, but I am quite sure that she's going to say yes. It's clear that they're crazy about each other. As happy as I am for them, watching them together only highlights how alone I am. It also makes me think of Ace, and I really don't want to be thinking about Ace. For someone who claimed to care for me, he made walking away look easy.

"You should call him," Teddy tells me on Tuesday evening. Fenn left half an hour ago, taking Noodle with her, and Teddy's been watching me pack. Jude is at *The Office*, getting things ready for his unexpected trip across the country.

"I wouldn't know what to say," I admit. I hold up a pale yellow shirt, and Teddy shakes her head.

I toss it on the discard pile and turn to find something else.

"You could start by telling him you made a mistake," she says gently.

"I don't think I did. He's been lying to me, Teddy."

"You don't know that."

"I know that he hasn't been telling the truth. And like dad says, omission of the truth is as good as a lie."

"I think after your big reveal, dad may have changed his mind about that."

"He's still not talking to me." I'd tried to call my father again this morning, but he'd let my mother answer.

"Look at the bright side. Once I get home and tell him I got drunk-married to a man he barely knows, your indiscretions will seem a lot less sordid."

I brighten. "That's true!"

Teddy laughs. "You could at least try to look less pleased about it. For my sake."

"He's going to love Jude. He already loves Jude. You'll be fine."

I pull out a few pastel tops and gather them in my arms.

"I better get going. I promised Jude I'd meet him for a drink,"

Teddy says. She gets up and gives me a meaningful stare. "Call him, Josie."

When she's gone, I slump onto the soft carpet and pull out my phone. I stare at Ace's name on the screen. My finger hovers over the call button. The phone pings with an incoming text and I almost drop it. *We need to talk.* It's from Alex. I stare at the words and a sob rises in my chest because it's not Alex I want to talk to right now. Decision made, I take a deep breath and dial Ace's number.

Ace answers on the first ring. "Josie?"

My courage evaporates.

"Josie, are you okay?" he sounds frantic.

"I'm fine."

"Oh, thank God."

"What's going on? Are you okay?" I ask, panicked.

"Hold on, give me a second." He mutes the phone, and I curse in frustration. It takes forever before he's back.

"What's wrong Josie? Why are you calling me?"

"I... I just wanted to talk."

"About?"

"About us."

I hear his shocked intake of breath. When he speaks again, he sounds stilted, as if he's trying to keep his temper in check. "What about us, Josie?"

He's agitated, and it's making me wish I'd never hit that call button.

"Never mind," I say quickly. "It was a mistake to call."

"You kicked me out," he says.

Without even thinking, the words pour out. "You said you'd come back."

He falls silent. I wait, cringing, the phone cradled against my ear.

"Do you want me to come back?"

That catches me off guard. "I don't know. I'm confused, Ace. I thought we... you just walked away, as if it meant nothing."

"Oh, Josie," he sighs, and I can hear the sincerity in his voice. "I was never far away."

What?

"What do you mean?"

He curses under his breath. I hear a man's voice, stern and berating. "Who are you with?" I ask.

"Hold on." He mutes me again, and I scream in frustration. "Josie, meet me downstairs."

Confusion, pure and simple, courses through me. I fly to my feet and out of my apartment. Has the elevator always been this slow? The lobby is empty. Frank smiles at me as I pass his station, and then I'm out the doors and on the sidewalk, scanning the street. Ace isn't here. A movement across the road draws my attention, and I frown in confusion as he steps out of the apartment block opposite mine. His face softens at the sight of me. His eyes never leave mine as he crosses the street.

"What are you doing here?" I ask when he's finally standing before me.

"Inside," he says. He's guarded, alert, and his shoulders are tense beneath his grey T-shirt. Behind him, through the door of his apartment block, I catch sight of a man standing just inside the door, watching us.

"Ace, you're freaking me out."

"Walk, Josie."

He follows me back inside. As soon as the elevator doors close, I let him have it.

"What the hell is going on? Who was that man? And why were you in that apartment block?"

"I'm going to lose my job for this," he replies.

"You don't have a job!"

"Let's get inside, Josie. I'll explain everything then."

We go to the living room. "Explain," I say.

Ace doesn't explain. Instead, he pulls a badge from his back pocket and hands it to me. I stare at the familiar crest. I've played an agent or two in my day. The seal is impossible not to recognize, nor is his name on the identity card beside it.

"FBI?" I whisper, my voice a croak. "Is this a joke?"

"No." he takes the badge back. "I'm going to hold onto this seeing as I'm about to lose it."

"You're with the FBI?" It's inconceivable.

"It's a long story, but yes."

"And you didn't tell me."

"I'm undercover, Josie. Not telling you is part of my job."

"But, why? Your being undercover has nothing to do with me – with us."

"My being undercover has everything to do with you."

A searing white pain shoots through my skull. "Oh, God."

Ace grabs my shoulders. "With you, Josie, not with us," he tries to explain, but it's too late. I yank out of his grasp.

"You needed me for a job, didn't you?"

"No, that's not what this is."

"Bullshit! What has this got to do with me?"

"It's complicated. For your own protection—"

"Don't you dare!" I roar. "I deserve to know!"

"Calm down!"

I slap him.

His head ricochets to the right. "Dammit Josie, calm down!" he yells just as his phone starts to ring.

"Hartley, this isn't a good time," he snaps. The person on the other end speaks rapidly, and the blood drains from Ace's face. "I've got her. Call it in, I want the full team ready to move." He ends the call and looks at me with real fear on his face. "Josie, listen to me. I don't have time to explain. You want to know why I'm here, why I've been watching you? It's Alex. This is all about Alex."

"Alex? Why on earth—"

"No time," he reminds me. "But you can't trust him, He's

dangerous, Josie. You said I used to be the good guy. I still am. Please, you have to trust me, and you have to trust me *now*."

"Why?" I croak.

"Because he's on his way up."

I barely have time to register his words when I hear the knock on the door. My blood turns to ice. Ace lifts a finger to his lips, warning me to be silent. My phone is still in my hand. I raise it to find another text from Alex, right after the last. *I'm coming over.* It must have come through while I was on the phone to Ace. I hold the phone up, and Ace reads the text.

"Just stay calm," he murmurs in my ear, "he's probably read about our break up and wants to try to get you back. Act natural, but get rid of him as soon as you can."

My heart is hammering in my chest, my saliva turned to acid.

"I'll be right here, Josie."

Another knock, louder this time. Ace slips into the kitchen and vanishes from sight. My feet are heavy as I walk toward the door.

"Hey." Alex smiles when he sees me, but it doesn't reach his eyes.

"Alex, what are you doing here?"

"I wanted to see you. I read about what happened." I don't ask whether he's referring to me having sex with Ace, or our break up. "Didn't you get my text?"

I shake my head. "It's not really a good time. I'm packing, I have an early flight."

"Chicago filming starting?" he asks fondly, reminding me that he knows my schedule as well as I do.

"Yes."

"Can I come in? I won't stay long." There's something different about his eyes. They're glittering, manic. After spending two years with Alex, I feel as though I'm looking at a stranger.

"I'm sorry, Alex, it's just not a good time." I start to close the door, but he rams his foot forward, jamming it open. I gape down at his shoe and then arch my brow.

"Alex?"

His smile changes. "I really do need to come in. I've done some digging, and I've discovered the most interesting facts about your new boyfriend. I assume *I'm* the reason he's been hanging around?"

"I don't know what you're talking about."

His eyes search my face, find the fear imprinted there. "You're a terrible actress."

A moment passes between us, one in which we both come to a decision. I throw my weight against the door. At the same time, Alex shoves it open. His superior strength wins out, and it bangs painfully into my shoulder.

"What has he told you?" Alex hisses in my ear. "What does he know?" His hand bites into my arm, jerking me toward him.

"Get your hands off me!"

"What, you don't like it rough?" he sneers. "You really had me fooled. All that time I held out for you, ever the gentleman, only for you to whore yourself to the next man to cross your path."

"Don't talk to me like that."

"I'll talk to you any way I damned well please. Now, you and I are going to sit down, and you're going to tell me *exactly* how much that bastard knows."

"And then what?"

His smile is pure malice, and a wave of nausea rises up in me. I try to shake him off with renewed energy, but he has me in a vice-grip. Desperate, terrified, I kick out at his shin. I'm barely able to appreciate the thud as my shoe connects, when he's hit me, hard, across the face. My vision swims, and I taste blood on my lip.

"Let her go." Ace's voice is a calm fury. He's standing in the kitchen doorway, his arm raised. The gun in his hand is trained on Alex, only an inch above my head. I feel Alex stiffen behind me. "Let her go," Ace repeats, taking a few steps toward us.

"Who the hell *are* you?" Alex asks, shifting so that I'm squarely between him and the gun.

Ace pulls out his badge. "John Logan, FBI. Now let her go."

"Not going to happen. Do you have any idea who I am? You're a dead man."

"Not yet, I'm not. And I know exactly who you are, you piece of shit. Now put the gun down and—"

Before Ace can finish speaking, Alex's free arm moves behind me. Too late, I call out a warning, but he's already pulled a gun. He presses it to my temple, the cold bite of steel nothing compared to the flare of terror in my chest. I let out a whimper.

"Drop it," Ace growls, his face a mask of fury. He takes another step toward us. Alex's only response is to twist the barrel more deeply into my skin.

"You first," Alex says. Ace falters.

"Don't!" I sob.

"Shut up!" Alex tells me. Then, glancing toward the door, he sidesteps, dragging me with him.

"You won't get away," Ace warns, keeping his voice level. "I have men stationed outside and at every exit."

"Please, Alex," I beg, "don't do this."

"I told you to shut up!"

He's so focused on me that he misses the quick look that Ace darts toward the door. It's still open, I realize. And the man that Ace spoke to on the phone – Hartley – knows Alex is here. If Ace told him to have the team ready to move, then that means...

I don't have time to think it through. Ace moves, launching forward as a gunshot rings out, so close to my ear, it's deafening. The boom renders me temporarily deaf as Alex jerks behind me, his arm tight around my throat. I see the glint of steel as he levels the gun. It all happens so fast, and then I'm screaming, watching helplessly as Ace drops to his knees and stares down at his chest in disbelief as blood blooms through his T-shirt.

A third gunshot and Alex's arm drops away. I lurch forward, falling to my knees beside Ace as men dressed in black pour into the room.

Ace is still conscious. I whip off my cardigan and press it to his chest to staunch the flow of blood. There's so much, my jeans are already soaked through.

"Ace!" I'm sobbing. His eyes meet mine, filled with relief.

"You're okay," he murmurs.

"Shhh, don't try to talk."

An agent appears on Ace's other side. He's yelling orders, calling for an ambulance. Firm hands pull me up, away from Ace. I kick out at the agent, but he steers me away. I twist in his grasp, see Ace speaking to the agent beside him. The man raises his hand. We stop. I'm free. I skid back to Ace's side. His smile is fading.

"Don't you dare die on me," I beg.

20

They let me ride in the ambulance, but I'm curled up in the far corner, staying out of the way while a team of paramedics works frantically to save Ace's life. Ace is so pale, deathly pale, and I keep my eyes fixed on the rise and fall of his chest. The agent who allowed me to stay – Ben Hartley, I learn – is with me, grim-faced.

"I told him not to go over there," he tells me. My heart pinches. If Ace hadn't been there, I don't know what Alex would've done, but I do know that Ace wouldn't have been hurt. "I don't need to tell you that this is confidential," Hartley says. I nod, not trusting myself to speak. "There's not much I can tell you, Miss Hudson, other than we've been investigating your ex-fiance for some time now. Let's just say he didn't make his money through corporate investments as he claims."

Past tense. Alex is dead. He was shot twice at close range. I should feel bad about it, but all I can think of is that he died too slowly. He managed to get a shot off at Ace before the team brought him down.

"How did he make his money, then?" I ask, even though I'm not sure I want to know the answer. Hartley casts a quick glance at the frantic medics.

"Not now," he murmurs, but I'm already distracted.

"Is he going to make it?" I whisper, gesturing at Ace.

"I've seen weaker men recover from worse."

They take Ace straight into surgery. I wait in the visitor's room, slumped in a straight-backed chair with my head in my hands. Black-clad strangers surround me, their collective concern palpable. They all know Ace so well – far better than I do, judging by the way they speak about him. I was so stupid. How did I not see that he was so much more than just a deadbeat wannabe actor?

"How long has Ace been an agent?" I ask the room at large. They all turn to look at me, seeming shocked to discover I'm there. A greying man with a scarred nose takes pity on me.

"Five years. He signed up right out of college and moved through the ranks faster than anyone else I know. It was just after his mother died."

His mother? I pull my phone from my purse and start to Google. It takes me a while, but I eventually find an article which mentions her, only briefly. Collateral damage of a drug bust gone wrong. *Jesus.* No wonder Ace dropped out and followed a career that would see justice served.

At some point, Hartley comes to stand before me. I see his black boots, but I don't look up.

"I'm going to need you to answer some questions, Miss Hudson."

"Josie," I say automatically.

"Josie," he acquiesces.

I lift my head. "Can it wait?"

He sighs and evicts the agent sitting beside me from his seat.

"Alex ran a drug cartel under cover of one of his subsidiaries. As far as we can gather, he's responsible for over a hundred million dollars' worth of heroin hitting U.S. soil in the past two years alone."

Drugs. Alex was dealing in drugs.

"How could I not know?" I spent two years with Alex, how could

I have been so blind to his crimes? I rack my brain, trying to think of a single instance that might have clued me in, but I come up blank. Barring the frequent travel, and the "meetings", which, admittedly, I never delved too deeply into, there was nothing out of the ordinary. No warning signs.

"He was a smart guy. Hell, it took us three years to build a case against him which might stick. And it gets worse. Over the past year, eight women have disappeared – prostitutes, runaways. Nobody paid much attention, until one of them managed to escape. The information she gave us led us to believe your husband was the abductor."

My mind reels. "Alex wasn't... he was never violent with me. Not once, in two years."

The look he gives me is pure pity. "Until he was," he says softly.

I blink back fresh tears. "Ace knew?"

"Yes. For what it's worth, Miss Hudson, I didn't want to bring you into this. I had no way of knowing whether you were involved in Mr. Masters' illegal activities. Logan went off plan when he contacted you."

"Why, though? Why contact me at all, why bring me into this mess?"

This time, the look he gives me is incredulous. "You really don't know the answer to that?"

"No, *Detective*, I really don't know the answer to that."

"Logan didn't want you tied up in this. He was concerned for your safety, especially when we discovered the missing women. He broke protocol when he made contact with you, to get you away from a man who is a suspected murderer. And he risked his badge to do it."

ACE SURVIVES THE SURGERY, but he's not out of the woods, not by a long shot. He's being monitored around the clock. No visitors are permitted, save for immediate family, and as far as I know, his father is still trying to find a flight out of Sacramento.

"You should go home and get some rest," Hartley tells me in the early hours of the morning. I'm slumped in my chair, and I have a plane to catch in six hours. He hands me a card with his contact details. "I'll have someone stationed outside your apartment until we're sure that all of Alex's accomplices have been brought to justice." He sees my longing glance down the hall. "You can come back tomorrow, perhaps they'll allow you in."

Reality asserts itself. "I'm supposed to be leaving for Chicago in a few hours."

"Can it wait?"

I stifle a sob. "I'm under contract."

"Well, I guess you've got to do what you've got to do. How soon can you get back?"

My mind draws a blank. I check the schedule on my phone, which is about to die.

"Not for at least ten days." Even then, I'll be pushing it. It'll have to be a day stop.

"He's going to need a long recovery, I'm sure he'll still be right here when you get back."

"I can't just leave him without even saying goodbye."

Hartley shrugs. I guess in a world of bullets and death, my feature film commitments must seem beyond trivial. I get to my feet, willing myself not to cry.

"I'll tell him you said goodbye," Hartley says. He doesn't meet my eyes when he says it.

21

Fenn is waiting in the lobby when I arrive home.

"Jojo!" She barrels into me, giving me the first real hug I've had since Ace left. I burst into tears. "I heard about the shooting. I've been desperate, but no one would give me any information and I couldn't get hold of Jude until just now..." she rattles this all off without pausing for breath. "He's on his way over, Teddy too. Oh my God, Jojo, I've been beside myself. What happened?"

"It's a really long story."

Fenn whips out her phone. "Reports are saying that Alex is dead."

"He is." I feel nothing when I say it. "I'm sorry, Fenn, but I can't tell you anything. There's an investigation and... well, I just can't say anything."

She shoves her phone back into her bag. "Understood. But you're okay?"

"I'm okay."

"What can I do?"

"Nothing, Fenn, honestly. All I need right now is a hot bath and to finish packing."

She steers me toward the elevator. "Well, I can help with that at least."

I'm soaking my weary bones in the sudsy water Fenn ran for me when Teddy barges into the bathroom, Jude hot on her heels.

I give a shriek of fright and try to cover myself with my face-cloth.

"What the hell happened?" Teddy asks furiously. Her lip is quivering and, before I can even get the words 'I'm okay' out of my mouth, she bursts into tears and drops to the floor beside the bath, drenching herself as she pulls me into a hug. I meet Jude's eyes over her shoulder. They're filled with concern.

"You okay?" He mouths the words. I nod as silent tears slide down my cheeks. Satisfied, he leaves the bathroom, closing the door quietly behind him. Teddy pulls herself together and helps me out of the bath. She dries my body, as gently as if I were a child, and then calls for Fenn to bring me something to wear. Ever-trustworthy Fenn brings me my most comfortable traveling outfit – soft jeans, sneakers and a cashmere sweater. I manage to dress myself, but that's as far as I get before I collapse onto my bed.

"I've put your phone on charge," Fenn says briskly, "and you're all packed."

Teddy gasps. "You're not seriously leaving?"

"Oh," Fenn adds, "and the press are here."

"Fucking bloodhounds," Jude growls, marching into my room in time to hear her last comment. "They've completely blocked the exit, Josie. You're not going anywhere for a while."

"I'm under contract," I whisper. The thing is, it doesn't sound like a big deal to anyone not in the know, but if I delay filming it costs the studio hundreds of thousands of dollars, which I'd be liable for. Not to mention the inconvenience to every single person who turns up. Not that I care about any of it, but this could ruin me. Legally, I have no choice but to go.

Fenn gives me a thoughtful look and darts out of the bedroom. A second later she's back with an enormous file. "There has to be a clause in your contract that covers extreme circumstances like this," she ponders out loud, flipping through the pages so fast it makes my head hurt. A tiny flame of hope flickers in my chest. I daren't let it kindle.

"George will know," I say. "He knows those contracts inside and out."

Fenn lifts her phone to her ear. "I'm on it," she says, striding out of the room.

Teddy sits down gently beside me and wraps both arms around my shoulders. "What happened?" she asks, keeping her voice down so only Jude can hear.

"Alex came over. He was bad news, Teddy. He..." my voice breaks and I feel her stiffen beside me.

"On a scale of one to ten, how bad?" she asks.

"There is no scale for people like him."

Jude curses. I manage a watery-eyed smile as I tell Teddy, "Jude never liked him."

Teddy doesn't smile back, but her grip tightens convulsively. "Did he hurt you?"

"No. He might have, but Ace stopped him."

"Ace?"

"I called him, like you told me to."

"No wonder the weather's all over the place. The last time you listened to me you were in kindergarten."

"It turns out Ace works for the FBI. They were investigating Alex this whole time."

"For what?"

I gaze helplessly at her. "I don't know what I'm allowed to say."

"Screw that. I'm your sister!"

"Leave it," Jude growls, uncharacteristically sharp with her. To my astonishment, Teddy takes a deep breath and leaves it.

"Where is Ace now?"

It's too much. I choke on my words. "He's in the hospital."

"The broadcast I saw mentioned an unidentified man was injured in the shooting," Jude says. "That was him?"

"Yes. He wouldn't even have been here if I hadn't—"

"Stop right there," Teddy cuts me off. "If he hadn't been here, you might've been hurt. Or worse. How bad is it?"

"He had surgery last night. He pulled through, but they wouldn't let me see him."

"George found a loophole!" Fenn bursts back into the room. "It's an unspecified clause, but he says in this instance it definitely applies." She pauses, catching sight of my stricken face. "He also said to tell you that if anyone gives you any shit about it, you let him know and he'll remind Garfield Harrison about the threesome in Cancun the night before his wedding." She shrugs. "I don't know if he means his or Harrison's wedding."

Despite everything, I smile through my tears. George always comes through. "I don't have to go?"

Fenn holds up the contract. "According to this, you may temporarily suspend filming for up to twenty-one days."

Three weeks. I leap off the bed and scramble for my sneakers.

"Where are you going?" Teddy squawks.

Jude is far more astute. "You're not going to make it through that crowd, Josie," he warns. I'd forgotten about them. I cock my head to one side and a small smile tugs up the corners of my mouth.

"Do you know how to ride a motorcycle?"

HARTLEY DOESN'T QUESTION why I want to know if Ace's bike is in the lot across the street. He even offers to have someone retrieve the keys from their base apartment. I don't know how much Ace has told him about me, but I gather he knows Ace wouldn't mind. The same man who followed me home and has been stationed outside my door jogs across to Ace's apartment block. The baying reporters barely give him a second look.

Ten minutes later, he pulls into the underground lot on Ace's bike. Jude gives me a wry look.

"Last chance to back out," he warns. "I'm more than a little rusty."

"I'm not changing my mind," I say. "The press sees what they want to. Jojo Hudson, Hollywood's darling would never be seen on the back of a motorcycle."

"Shows how little they know," Jude grins. "Because Josie Hudson, my favorite waitress, has got a lot more backbone."

I climb up behind him, and he guns the engine. I only have time to wrap my arms around his waist, and we're off, speeding up the ramp and out onto the street. I sneak a glimpse at the pack of reporters outside my apartment doors, baying for blood. Nobody pays us any attention, except for a lone, mousy-haired man a few feet away. I flip him the bird as Jude leans us into a corner and we disappear into the traffic.

22

My sneakers make no sound on the clinical white tiles. I feel a bit ridiculous carrying a helmet over my arm, but I'm so thrilled that we managed to evade the press, I don't even care. In fact, I might start biking everywhere.

Hartley is the only one left in the visitor's lounge. He gets to his feet when we walk in. "Miss Hudson?" His eyes fall to the helmet. "I guess you got hold of that bike, although I must admit I didn't expect to see you back here so soon."

"I found a loophole in my contract. How is he?"

"He's awake, or so the doctors tell me."

"Can we see him?"

"Not yet. I'm going to stick around until they give us the go ahead."

I take my familiar seat. "Well then, I'm waiting with you."

Jude brings us coffee from the machine down the hall.

"You should go," I tell him after the second cup. "Teddy will be worried. I'll call you if I need you to come back."

He hesitates, torn between wanting to stay with me, wanting to see Teddy, and wanting to escape the monotony of the hospital. I also think he's itching to get back on the bike, although he'd never admit it.

"You're sure?" he asks eventually.

"I'm sure."

"Okay." He gets to his feet. "You call me the second you want to leave and I'll come back and get you."

Hartley listens to our conversation without saying a word. Until Jude leaves.

"He the bartender?" he asks.

I imagine a board filled with black and white surveillance photographs and wonder just how much of my life this man has witnessed. "He is," I reply.

"Logan likes him. Says he's a good guy."

A movement at the doorway has us both on our feet, but it's not the surgeon. It's Ace's father. Even though I've never met him, the resemblance is impossible to miss.

"Mr. Logan." Hartley offers his hand, but Ace's dad pulls him into a bear hug instead.

"Ben. Thank you for calling me. How is he?"

"He's not in any immediate danger, but he's not out of the woods yet, either. We're expecting another update any minute now."

"Have you seen him?"

"No, Sir."

Ace's dad nods. His eyes fall to me.

"This is Jojo Hudson," Hartley begins, but Ben's dad holds up a hand to stop him.

"I know who she is." He takes two long strides toward me. "It's Josie, right?" he asks. I swallow the lump which has formed in my throat and bob my head. His eyes twinkle as he pulls me into a hug. "I wondered when I'd meet the girl who stole my son's heart," he says in my ear. Then, pulling back to look into my eyes, "I only wish it was under better circumstances." I start to laugh, dazzled by the fact that Ace told his dad about me, but it turns into a sob. "Oh, none of that now, girl," Mr. Logan says, pulling me back to his shoulder and thumping my back in what I assume is supposed to be a soothing gesture. "Logan men are made of strong stuff. You better toughen up if you expect to be with one."

I hiccup against his broad chest. "Yes, Sir," I mumble.

"It's Robert," he insists.

He finally lets me go when the surgeon arrives. I swipe at my eyes and nose, my face burning.

"Mr. Logan, I'm Doctor Thompson," he says, shaking Robert's hand. "I assume you've been brought up to date?"

"How is my son?" Robert asks, cutting through the preamble.

The Doctor smiles. "I don't like to make early predictions, but I think it's safe to say he's going to make a full recovery." He's barely finished speaking when Robert treats him to his own bear hug, lifting him clear off his feet. He doesn't seem to know what to do and flops around like a rag doll.

Once he's back on solid ground, he turns to Hartley. "I've moved him, as you requested. He's in a private ward. I'm sorry it took so long, but moving equipment out of ICU isn't as easy as it sounds."

"I appreciate everything you've done," Hartley replies.

"It's the least we can do, given the circumstances."

I blink at them in alarm. Hartley notices me and lowers his voice. "It's just a precaution, while he's incapacitated. I'll have a man stationed permanently outside his door."

"Can we see him?" Robert asks.

The Doctor hesitates, but Hartley clears his throat audibly, reminding him that this is not just any patient. I assume allowances are made for Federal agents who risk their lives for country.

"Of course," he replies smoothly. "But only one visitor at a time."

We follow him down the hall, through a labyrinth of twists and turns, until we reach a non-descript door.

"One at a time," the doctor reminds us, before returning to his rounds.

Robert goes first. He's inside a long time, and he's already apologizing on his way out.

"He's fallen asleep," he whispers.

Hartley sweeps a practiced look up and down the hallway and then pushes the door open. "Come on," he tells me with a jerk of his head. I don't need to be told twice. I slip inside, and he follows.

Ace is fast asleep, attached to so many machines it takes me a while to navigate my way to his side. Hartley settles for standing straight-backed at the foot of the bed. Ace's face is so pale even his blond hair looks dark. I find my eyes drawn to the bandage around his chest and my heart pinches. We stand in silence, watching over him. I'm happy just to look at him, but I suspect Hartley has no desire to examine every inch of his precious face because after ten minutes he excuses himself. At the soft sound of the door closing, Ace opens his eyes.

"I thought he'd never leave," he wheezes, a flash of mischief in his dulled eyes.

"You're awake!" I want to throw myself on him, to hug him, but it's impossible with all the electrodes covering his chest. I settle for taking his hand.

"Only just. I should've stopped him, but I wanted to talk to you alone first."

The word 'alone' makes me feel warm and fuzzy. "I was so worried about you," I say, "I didn't know if you were going to make it."

"Such little faith in me," he teases. Then he turns serious. "Alex?"

"He's gone."

"I'm sorry."

"For what?"

"I know he meant a lot to you."

"Not as much as I thought." Carefully, I take a seat on the very edge of the bed. "I can't believe I didn't suspect anything. All those terrible things he was doing and I was completely oblivious."

"You need to know that I didn't set out to ruin your life, Josie. I knew you were dating him, obviously. The whole world knew that, but it wasn't until he came under investigation for murder and abduction that I decided to do anything about it." I stay silent. "You should also know," he begins slowly, "that I have absolutely zero interest in becoming an actor."

I start to laugh and find I can't stop. "So you don't need me to advance your career after all?"

"I don't need you to advance my career." A pause, and then he says the sweetest words I've ever heard. "But I do need *you*."

"I need you too."

We lapse into a beautiful silence, our hands the only physical contact between us.

"Hey," Ace says after a while, "aren't you supposed to be flying out today?"

A grin splits my face as I recall how we started, and the road that brought us here. "I didn't get on the plane," I say meaningfully. Ace's answering smile is the sun coming out from behind a dark cloud.

"You didn't get on the plane," he echoes.

Screw it, I think, leaning toward him. I hear the electronic tempo of his heartbeat spike as our lips meet. By the time Doctor Thompson bursts through the door, a grinning Hartley behind him, neither of us is in any state to notice.

THE END

ABOUT THE AUTHOR

Rachel Rhodes is a pseudonym for award-winning author, copywriter, and lover of the written word, Melissa Delport. She is published in both S.A and the U.S.A and offers professional copywriting services and author coaching.

For ten years she owned and operated her own specialized logistics company until she woke up one morning and decided it was time to put her English degree to good use.

Melissa lives with her husband and three teenagers, none of whom take her seriously.

She also writes romantic suspense as Lissa Del and contemporary romance as Rachel Rhodes.

For more information, visit www.melissadelport.com

ALSO BY RACHEL RHODES

ROMANCE & ROMANTIC COMEDY (as Rachel Rhodes)

Awkward in Print

Awkward Abroad

Awkward Infidelity

Awkward in Trouble

CONTEMPORARY WOMENS FICTION (as Lissa Del)

Rainfall

Riven

A Life Made of Lava

URBAN FANTASY

GUARDIANS OF SUMMERFELD SERIES

The Cathedral of Cliffdale (Book 1)

The Fight of the Fallen (Book 2)

The Hope of Hawkstone (Book 3)

The Balance of the Blood (Book 4)

Full Series Boxed Set (Books 1-4)

SHADOW MAGIC SERIES

The Witchborn Curse (Book 1)

The Shadow Huntress (Book 2)

The Charmed Quarter (Book 3)

The Rogue Coven (Book 4)

The Darkest Realm (Book 5)

The Hybrid's Fate (Book 6)

Full Series Boxed Set (Books 1-6)

THE TRAVELER DUOLOGY

The Traveler (Book 1)

The Survivor (Book 1.5)

The Saviour (Book 2)

TIME TRAVEL FANTASY

The Clock Keeper

DYSTOPIAN

THE LEGACY TRILOGY

The Legacy (Legacy Trilogy Book 1)

The Legion (Legacy Trilogy Book 2)

The Legend (Legacy Trilogy Book 3)

ANTHOLOGIES

The Space Between Dreams & Chaos

The Space Between Magic & Mayhem

www.ingramcontent.com/pod-product-compliance
Lightning Source LLC
Chambersburg PA
CBHW020912310726
48980CB00011B/855/J

* 9 7 8 0 6 3 9 8 4 4 8 5 5 *